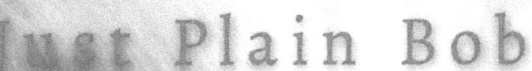

Just Plain Bob

7 INTENSE
STORIES IN 1

She
MAKES ME...

EROTICA SHORT STORIES, VOL. 16

WARNING

This book contains sexually explicit scenes and adult language. It may be considered offensive to some readers. This book is for sale to adults ONLY.

Please store your files wisely where they cannot be accessed by underage readers.

* * * * * * * * * * * * * * * * * * *

WANT FREE COPIES OF MY BOOKS?

Just visit my blog and download free copies of my books:

awesomeauthors.org/justplainbob

About the Publisher

4Fun Publishing, a member of **BLVNP Incorporated**, 340 S. Lemon #6200, Walnut CA 91789, info@blvnp.com / legal@blvnp.com
NOTE: Due to the highly emotional reaction of some people to works of erotic fiction, any email sent to the above address that contains foul language or religious references is automatically deleted by our anti-spam software and will not be seen. All other communications are welcome.

DISCLAIMER

Erotica Short Stories, Vol. 16

She Makes Me...

7 Intense Stories in 1

By: Just Plain Bob

© **Just Plain Bob 2015**
ISBN: 978-1-68030-339-1

Table of Contents

Aimee

I knew that I had seen her some place before. As I watched her walk around the room I racked my brain to try and remember where and when it had been. If what she said was true, and I had no reason to doubt her, I couldn't possibly have seen her someplace else. Until then she had never left California and I had never been in that state, but I still would have bet every dime I had that I had seen her before.

The call had come as a complete surprise. "Hey bro, stop by mom and dad's after work tonight. I've got someone I want you to meet."

"When did you get back in town?"

"This morning. I figured things might be pretty dull around here so I came home to shake things up. Got to run bro, got lots more calls to make. See you tonight."

Teddy had graduated with a degree in Electrical Engineering and had promptly split for California to take a job with one of the Silicon Valley computer firms. The last time I had talked with him he was singing the praises of that part of the world and he had left me with the impression that he was never going to leave that state and go anywhere where there was one minute less sunshine. I spent the rest of that day wondering what could possibly bring him home.

What happened was Aimee. Aimee was the embodiment of the term 'California Beach Bunny'. Tall, tanned, long honey blond hair that hung to the middle of her back and a body built for the specific purpose of driving the male sex wild. Ted introduced us and then said, "Aimee and I are getting married."

Lucky bastard I thought even as I looked at her and thought that

I had seen her someplace. You know how it is when you meet someone you think you've met before or seen some place? It crawls inside your head and stays with you as you drive yourself bananas trying to remember. She noticed my attention and she came over to me.

"Is there a sign on my back that says 'kick me' or are you staring at me because you are enthralled with my beauty?"

"Enthralled of course. That and the fact that I would swear on a stack of Bibles that I've seen you some place before now."

"When was the last time you were in California?"

"I've never been there."

"Well this is my first trip out of the state so I have no idea where we could have run across each other."

"Curious, but the feeling is there and it will eat on me until I resolve it, at least in my mind."

She shrugged and moved away to talk to somebody else and I went to find Teddy.

"Where are you staying while you are here?"

At the Best Western off Meadows and Founders Parkway."

"Bullshit bro. I'm sitting in an almost empty three-bedroom house and I could use the company. It gets lonely in that big place."

"Why don't you sell it? The place can't have much in the way of good memories for you."

"It is my revenge bro. The divorce decree gives Lisa half when I sell it, but not until I sell it and the decree doesn't set a time limit. If I live there for fifty years it means that cheating whore doesn't get a dime for fifty years. When we leave tonight we will swing by the Best Western and pick up your stuff. Tell Aimee not to worry. The house is so well built that it is almost sound proof. The two of you can raise all kinds of hell and I'll never hear a thing."

The party was running down and Ted and Aimee went to get their coats and as we were heading for the door Aimee dropped her purse and bent down to pick it up. When she did her blouse rode up in the back and I saw the tattoo. It was intricate scrollwork about twelve inches long and maybe six inches high and as soon as I saw it the penny dropped and I knew where I had seen Aimee. I'd have to wait until I got home to make absolutely sure, but there really wasn't any doubt in my mind. When Aimee stood up she saw me looking at her and she read my facial expression and her facial expression told me what she saw – "He knows."

We made small talk on the way to the motel and then on the way to my house. Ted pointed out the local sites as we drove along, but Aimee was mostly quiet. She kept glancing over at me as if expecting that I would suddenly shout, "I know where it was that I saw you" and then proceed to tell Teddy. When we got to my place I showed them to their room and then I gave Aimee a tour of the place so she would know where to find things and then I bid them goodnight. I went to the living room and read until they had time to fall asleep and then I got up and headed for my home office. I booted up the computer, got on the Net and then logged onto one of my favorite sites. I went searching through the index until I found the section I was looking for, brought it up and there she was. Absolutely no doubt about it. The name on the clip was Lois, but it was sure enough Aimee.

I heard the door open and close behind me and I turned and saw Aimee standing there. "You know, don't you?"

I nodded a yes.

"All of it?"

Again I nodded a yes and pointed to the monitor where a clip from GangBang Squad was playing out. Aimee was on her knees inside a circle of five black men with large cocks and she was taking turns at sucking them. She looked over my shoulder, "I knew when I saw your face as we were leaving that you had figured it out. Not exactly my proudest moment."

"Maybe not, but you sure look good doing it."

"I was out of a job, the rent was due and I hadn't eaten in two days. I was really hurting for money when a guy I knew asked me if I would be interested in making fifteen hundred for something I usually did on weekend nights for free and I said yes. Only it wasn't like what I did on weekend nights. All I did then was pick out a cute guy and have some fun. I didn't know it was a bunch of black guys until I got there."

"Why didn't you leave?"

She shrugged, "I just said it. I was out of a job, the rent was due and I hadn't eaten in two days."

She pointed at the monitor, "You spend much time on that looking for porn?"

"Quite a bit. It is my sexual outlet since my wife left me for a couple of bikers."

"Then you will probably come across me again. After the gangbang I did a couple more to keep the money coming in until I could find a job. I did one for MILF Seekers, one for Her First Big Cock, one for Her First Anal and two for Suck Bus. You going to tell Teddy?"

"Of course not. He's happy, you seem happy, why should I screw things up for the two of you? I do have a question though."

"What?"

"I know how big Ted is in the cock department. You going to be happy with him in bed after all those huge cocks I've seen you take?"

"I won't lie. Big is good. Hell, big is great, but there is more to a marriage than just sex. Ted is very good in bed and as long as the love, affection, and caring are there what he has will be more than enough."

"Then I guess you should have a happy life because Ted has always given a hundred percent in everything that he does."

"Yes, well, I just have to make sure that he gets the chance to do it," she said as she moved toward me.

"What are you doing?"

"I'm not a very trusting person," she said as she took off her blouse. "You say you won't tell Ted, but blood will tell and you might just decide that your brother shouldn't marry a slut who loves huge black cocks." Her bra hit the floor as she reached me and knelt down on the floor between my legs. She reached for my zipper and pulled it down.

"A little reverse blackmail here. I'm going to suck your cock and then I'm going to fuck your eyes out. You won't be able to tell Ted anything without outing yourself."

"This is not a wise move Aimee. You said that Ted would be enough for you and I believe you."

"I also said big was great and you can tell from what's on the screen how big a slut I can be when I have big black cocks rooting around in my holes. You just might start thinking that I'll backslide and decide not to take a chance on letting your little brother marry a black cock loving whore."

She had my cock out and was stroking it and I wasn't trying all that hard to fight her off. I remembered how she looked sliding up and down on a large piece of black meat and how she sounded when she screamed, "Oh fuck yeah, oh yeah, fuck me, oh sweet Jesus fuck my pussy." No way I could have a soft cock after that.

"You said that like you still are one."

"I am brother in law to be, I am. I love it, I crave it and I always will, but I love Ted enough that I'll give it up when we are married."

"You haven't given it up yet?"

Aimee gave a little chuckle and said, "What do you think?" as her mouth closed around my cock.

End of the 1st Story

Alisha

My wife Alisha is a slut, but I can't complain because she was a slut when I met her, she was a slut the whole time I dated her and putting a ring on her finger didn't change a thing.

It was my cousin Lou's bachelor party and there were eleven of us and we were drinking booze, watching porno films and waiting for the stripper I had hired. The doorbell rang and when I answered the door I found a young lady standing there. She was wearing blue jeans, and overcoat, tennis shoes and her hair was tucked up under a blue navy watch cap. She didn't look a day over fourteen and I thought she must have been selling Girl Scout cookies or something.

"Can I help you?"

She grinned at me, "No, I'm here to help you" and she bent down and picked up a boom box that I hadn't noticed. "Got a place where a girl can change? Or do you want me to do it in jeans and tennis shoes?"

I showed her to the bedroom and she handed me the boom box, "It's ready to go. Give me five minutes and then press the play button."

I was right on the ragged edge of asking her for some ID, but at the last minute I decided that the agency I'd hired her through wouldn't hire anyone under age. I waited the five minutes and then I hit the play button, the music started, the bedroom door opened and oh what a difference five minutes could make. High heels, a red peignoir covering an almost non-existent bikini and a body that looked to be 36-22-36 and solid. Her long black hair was in a ponytail that hung down to her ass and it flew around like a whip as she gyrated around the room. It took her five minutes to do her strip tease and when she was done there wasn't a soft cock in the place. The guys didn't want her to leave and I told them I would see what I could do. I approached Alisha and told her the guys wanted her to stay and she said very matter of factly, "I get fifty bucks for a lap dance. A blow job is seventy-five and a half and half is a hundred and a quarter. How many guys are here?" I told her and she thought for a minute and then said, "I'll do the whole bunch for eighteen hundred."

I told the guys and before I even finished the price list they had their wallets out. It was the wildest thing I'd ever seen. She did a lap dance for Lou that ended up with her sitting on his cock while another one of the guys stood in front of her and fed his cock into her mouth. After Lou got his rocks off everyone retired to the bedroom where Alisha took on everyone, one, two and even three at a time. It was six in the morning before the last exhausted guy staggered out the front door leaving a very fucked out Alisha lying on my bed. She looked up at me, "Well, was your party a success?"

I smiled at her, "Thanks to you I don't believe anyone who was here will ever forget it. The biggest problem is that now Lou isn't so sure he wants to get married. He's quite taken with you."

She laughed, "Well, I am looking for a husband and I haven't had much luck."

"Why not? You're gorgeous and you are fantastic in bed and while I know there needs to be a little more to a relationship than just that at least you have that much of a head start."

"Whoever marries me will have to put up with me doing what I did last night. Not too many men around who could handle that, could you?"

I just stared at her as I considered what she'd said. She took my silence to mean agreement and said, "There, see what I mean?"

I grinned at her, "Don't rush me, I'm thinking, I'm thinking. Maybe we should talk about this over breakfast. Why don't you take a shower while I go see what's in the cupboard. How do you like your eggs?"

Alisha was twenty-three and had been working as a stripper for almost four years and selling sex for almost as long. There wasn't any long, involved story behind it - she loved to fuck! She had been giving it away since she was old enough to know what it was that she had; she had developed a liking for multiple partners and that had led to a gangbang or two, but it had never been for money. She had started stripping as an accident. She was in college and was looking for a part time job. Her roommate in the dorm worked for an agency doing singing telegrams and told Alisha that the agency was always looking for new talent. Alisha had applied, taken an audition and was hired. She had been on the job for about five months when she was called into the office and asked if she could dance. The agency had gotten into a bind; they had eight bookings for strippers, but only had six strippers available. Alisha said she would give it a try.

It was a small bachelor party, only nine guys, and she had done her dance and was getting ready to leave when one of the guys asked her if she would do something "special" for the groom to be. He offered her two hundred bucks to give the man a lap dance and a blow job and she had agreed to do it. Before the night was over she had sucked and fucked every man there and had gone home with eleven hundred dollars in her purse, not counting what the agency paid her. She had thought that the dancing would be a one-time thing, but the guy who had put on the party had called the agency and told them how pleased they were with Alisha. The agency had asked Alisha if she would like to be added to their list of dancers and she had said yes.

Alisha didn't always charge for sex. If she got to a party and like the looks of the crowd they sometimes got her for free. Granted - it didn't happen often, but it did happen. The bottom line was that Alisha found out that she could make money for doing what she was willing to do for free. I have to admit that sitting across the table from her I was both captivated by her looks and fascinated by her story and even though I had seen what a slut she was I wanted to get to know her better. On an impulse I asked her to have dinner with me some night and she said, "Why in the world would you want to do something like that?"

To be truthful, I didn't really know, but I grinned at her and said, "How are you going to find a husband if you don't date?"

She gave me a very strange look, "Knowing what you know you're wanting to date me?"

"What can I say? I've already told you that as far as I'm concerned you have a head start. I'd just like to see what else you got."

***

Most men (and women for that matter) would consider the next six months as rather strange. Alisha and I dated on the nights she didn't work and on the nights she did I sat home knowing that she was somewhere being fucked. A month after we started dating she stopped by my apartment one night after one of her jobs and asked me if I was still a prospective husband. I told her that I was considering it and she said, "The man who marries me is going to have to be willing to eat my pussy after other men have fucked me. Do you think you can do that?"

To be honest I really didn't think that I could, but she asked me to at least try. I looked at her lying on the bed, legs spread and her cunt hair looking like a white matted mess and I almost turned away. She noticed the hesitation and started to get up.

"You almost had me believing," she said, "But I always knew that no man could take me the way I am."

Be brave I thought to myself and I pushed her back down onto the bed. My stomach was turning, but I knew that it was mostly mental. It was slimy goo with no discernable taste except for being salty and I found that I didn't mind eating her at all and she seemed to love it. After several minutes she pulled me up and said, "Thanks lover, now let me give you your reward" and she spent the rest of the night trying to fuck my brains out. When we finally reached the point where she couldn't get me up anymore she snuggled up against me and said, "You know, we might even be able to make this work."

Shortly after that Alisha moved in with me and my eating her pussy after her "dates" became part of our love making routine. By the end of six months I was asking her to marry me and to her credit she kept refusing me.

"I know you think you know what you are getting into, but you don't. No one man can ever keep me sexually satisfied. You would be looking at fifty years of me fucking other guys and sooner or later you would get fed up with it. And what about your relationship with your family and friends? How would you handle them knowing that you were married to me? Don't forget, I fucked a bunch of them at your cousin's bachelor party. You think that once we are married they won't be constantly hitting on me behind your back and that I won't fuck them? You think their girlfriends and wives won't find out about me and avoid me like the plague. Can you see yourself taking me to Christmas dinner at your relative's house and having them turn their backs on the whore you brought home? Just leave it be baby. It's working for us just like it is and this way when you do get fed up with the bullshit you can just walk away without having to do all that divorce crap."

She was right of course, on almost all of it, but I loved her and I did love living with her and I convinced myself I needed to marry her. I needed to marry her just to prove to her how much I loved her. It took me another six months to wear her down, but even then she had conditions before she would agree to say yes.

"Since the word is going to go out to your family and friends anyway that you married a whore, we are going to speed up the process. I'm going to be the entertainment at your bachelor party and you are going to eat me in front of everybody when they are through with me. I'm going to be the biggest slut they have ever seen and they are going to see that you know it and don't care."

I know she laid those conditions on me expecting me to refuse, but I surprised her and agreed.

"But it works both ways baby. If I do what you say you have to marry me - no backing out. Deal?"

She shook her head yes and I dragged her off to bed.

***

There were twenty-one guys at my bachelor party and they were split pretty evenly - half family and half friends. My two brothers and four of my cousins had been at Lou's bachelor party and I was sure they would remember Alisha and so would about half of my friends. So far Lou was the only one present who knew that Alisha was the bride to be. Where my family was concerned only my mom and dad had met her. For the rest of them my lifting of her veil at the wedding would be the first they would know of it. By the time Alisha and I got to the reception the word would be out and everyone would know. It would be an interesting evening.

As far as the bachelor party went Alisha started out by doing a strip tease that had steam coming out of everyone's ears. Then I had to sit on a chair as she did a lap dance for me which led to her kneeling between my legs and sucking my cock. Then she stood up, turned her back to me, straddled me and sat on my cock. She started moving up and down and my brother Todd stepped in front of her and offered her his cock and she bent forward and took it. From there on it was pure orgy as Alisha took on everybody there two and three at a time. By midnight every one there had fucked her at least three times and Alisha called a halt to the proceedings.

"Everyone can stick around for more if you want it but I have something that I have to do first. I am a slut, an absolute slut! I fuck because I love to fuck, but there is some one here tonight who is even more of a slut than I am. He is a cum slut and I have a wedding present for him."

She crooked a finger at me and I walked over to her and she pointed at the floor and I lay down on my back. Cum was running out of her pussy in gobs as she lowered herself onto my face and then she said, "Who want's their dick sucked while he's eating me?"

The party lasted three more hours and then Alisha and I went back to my apartment where I ate her again.

***

The gasps were very loud when I lifted Alisha's veil to kiss her after the "I do's" and I was certain that by the time Alisha and I got to the hall that everyone there would know about Alisha and the bachelor party. It became very clear who our friends were going to be by watching who came up to talk to us and who shied away. Interestingly enough, at least to me, almost all of the married women talked to Alisha while the single ones stayed away. Later on during the honeymoon Alisha told me that three of them - she wouldn't tell me who - wanted to know all about the bachelor party. And almost all of the married women invited her to call on them when we got back from our honeymoon and settled in. When it was time for me to remove her garter and toss it to the single guys I decided to be naughty and when I reached up under Alisha's wedding gown I grabbed her panties and pulled them down. Just before I threw them over my shoulder I noticed that the crotch was wet with cum stains. I looked up at her and saw her smiling at me, "Tell you later" she whispered. Ten minutes later, when we were dancing together, she told me that every guy who had been at the party had asked when they could see her again. "I gave them our room number at the hotel and invited them up. You don't mind, do you? I promise that after I do them and you eat my pussy, I won't fuck anyone but you during the rest of the honeymoon, okay?"

What the hell, I knew what I was getting into when I signed on so I just said, "Okay, but what about the cum stained panties?"

She giggled, "Both of your brothers said they couldn't get away from their wives to come to the hotel so I fucked them in the coat closet."

That was ten years ago and Alisha still dances at parties and then takes money for the sex that usually follows. At least once a week she does a gangbang at the house and sometimes I participate, but I usually watch and wait for the chance to eat her pussy when she is done. I'm getting cream pies almost every night of the week and in return Alisha does her very best to try and fuck me to death. Believe me, it's not a bad life.

The End

Curious Lorrie

Lorrie and I had been married for almost fifteen years and it was a good marriage. We loved each other and we were also each other's best friend. We were a typical middle class couple. We both worked at fairly decent jobs and had typical outside activities. I bowled on Wednesday night, played poker a couple of times a month with friends, and played golf almost every weekend that Lorrie and I didn't take the boat and go to the lake. Lorrie played cards with her sorority sisters from college every Thursday night, volunteered for charity work one or two nights a week and, I'm almost ashamed to say, whipped my ass on the golf course on the non-lake weekends. We made ourselves a promise when we got married that we would not become stay at home couch potatoes. We moved in a circle that believed in having parties, barbecues and in entertaining. We belonged to the Benevolent and Protective Order of Elks, more for the weekly dances than for any other reason and, in short; we were a very happy and active couple.

One day, out of the blue, Lorrie asked, "Do you ever think about other women?"

"Do I what?"

"You know, see other women and wonder what they would be like?"

"Yes, I suppose so."

"What do you think about when you see them?"

"I don't know, it's never the same thing. I'll see a woman with great legs and I'll wonder what she would look like wearing four-inch heels. Or I'll see a woman with large breasts and I'll wonder what she would look like in a bustier, a push up bra or just letting them hang free."

"Do you ever think about taking them to bed?"

"Yes and no."

"Explain that please."

"I sometimes try to imagine what they would be like, but I never actually think about trying to bed one of them. Why?"

"I don't really know. Just trying to get a feel for the male mind I suppose."

"I know you Lorrie, there has to be more to it than that."

Lorrie was silent for several moments and then she said, "At the card game last night Lisa did some crying on my shoulder. Dave is out screwing other women. Lisa said he has always liked looking at the ladies and she had always just accepted it as being the way guys are. You know, look but no touching? Only now all of a sudden Dave is out there touching. I just wondered what it was."

"Well babe, looking is human nature and so is lusting, but if you have a good marriage there is no reason to go touching. What is Lisa going to do about it?"

"Her attitude is "What's good for the goose is good for the gander. She has started going out with other guys."

"I raised an eyebrow at that, "I always thought they were a happy couple. Their marriage must not be as good as I thought."

"I don't know. She says she still loves him and she's pretty sure that he still loves her."

It was about two months later when Lorrie hit me with the question that makes most men cringe, "Do you love me? I mean really,

really love me?"

"Of course I do."

"You do know that I love you too, don't you?"

"Yes."

"Well I do. I just hope you love me as much as needed."

"What's wrong Lorrie, why the questions?"

Lorrie looked down at the floor and said, "I've been having an affair."

I couldn't have been more surprised if Lorrie had told me that she had just robbed a bank. I was stunned and at a loss for words and it was several seconds before I managed to squeak out, "How long has it been going on?"

"About a month now."

"With who?"

"You don't know them."

"Them? Good God Lorrie, what are you doing, gangbangs?"

"No, no, that came out wrong. I didn't see them both at the same time. I guess what I meant to say is that I've been having affairs, not an affair."

I was still recovering from the initial shock and I didn't know what to say or what to do, so to buy time I said, "You had better start at the beginning Lorrie and tell me just what the hell is going on."

It had started when Lisa began confiding in Lorrie about what was going on in her life. Dave's running around was the best thing that had ever happened to her. She started playing the field and the more men she dated the more fun she had. She'd had no idea that men were so different when it came to sex. Cocks in all sizes and shapes, circumcised and not, different ways of making love and so on. She told Lorrie that she had the best of both worlds - a husband (though a straying one) who loved her and the sexual excitement of new lovers. Lisa began working on Lorrie to try another man. Lorrie said she couldn't, but Lisa kept after her. Lisa told her about the men she had been with and how each one had brought something different into the affair.

One night after cards Lisa's car wouldn't start so Lisa asked Lorrie to drive her over to the lounge where she was supposed to meet her current lover. When they got there Lisa didn't see her lover's car and so she asked Lorrie to come inside and keep her company while she waited. The two of them had three or four drinks before Lisa's lover arrived and when he did show up he had a friend with him. As the men approached Lisa leaned over and told Lorrie that the guy with her boyfriend was Troy and that he had the biggest cock she had ever seen.

Lorrie had just enough alcohol in her to be in a mellow so when the two guys sat down she didn't get up and leave. She sat there and talked with Lisa and her friends and when Troy asked her to dance she hadn't seen any reason not to. On the dance floor Troy kept poking his cock into her leg and it felt huge. She wondered what it looked like and she got to thinking about what I had said when I told her what I sometimes imagined when I saw a woman with large breasts. She started imagining what Troy's cock would look like in boxers, in jockey shorts or in Speedo style briefs. She wondered what it would look like hanging free - would it hang down to his knee or maybe only go to mid-thigh. She was daydreaming about stuff like that when Troy kissed her. She automatically returned the kiss and when he gave her some tongue she gave some back and then suddenly she snapped out of her daydream and broke from him, but the damage had been done.

Troy just knew that he had a hot one on the line. He worked on Lorrie until she finally had enough and she got up to leave. Troy insisted on walking her out to her car and when they got to it he said, "Just so you'll know what you missed out on, look at this." He had taken his cock out of his pants and he stood there stroking it and watching Lorrie's face. It was huge and it seemed to mesmerize her and she couldn't take her eyes off of it. After several seconds Troy had taken her hand and put it on his dick and the two of them stood there in the parking lot - Troy watching Lorrie and Lorrie standing there staring at the huge piece of meat in her hand. They stood there what seemed like forever and then Troy had slowly lifted his hands, put them on Lorrie's shoulders and gently pushed her down and then Troy's cock was in her mouth and then she was in the back seat.

For the next three weeks she had seen him two or three times a week before breaking off with him. "If his cock was so good why did you quit seeing him?"

"Because he was an asshole. All he was was a huge cock. He had no finesse or anything else going for him. He had a big dick and I was supposed to be grateful that he was letting me have it. He was a novelty and he quickly wore off. What he did do for me was to make me curious."

"How so?"

"I began to understand what Lisa was trying to tell me about the sexual excitement of a new man. I had fucked Troy, but he meant nothing to me. His huge cock didn't make me stop loving you, if anything all Troy did was make me appreciate you even more. No, what he did was make me curious about other men. The next Thursday Lisa asked me if I was meeting Troy later and I told her no, that I'd dropped him. She said that she had expected it and that two weeks of him was all she could stand. Then she told me that she had someone else she wanted me to meet and that night she introduced me to Mack. Mack was totally different from Troy and you. His cock was just a bit shorter than yours and it was skinny - like a hot dog, but what he lacked in size he more than made up for in energy. He was like the Energizer Bunny, he kept going and going and going. His big thing was anal sex and it was the first time I ever had a cock up my butt and I liked it. I saw him for two weeks, but I broke off with him day before yesterday because he was getting too possessive."

"So why in God's name did you tell me all this shit? You had two affairs, you ended both of them, I never knew and never suspected and you could have kept quiet and it would never have become the problem that it is now going to be. Why didn't you just keep quiet?"

"Try to understand this John. I love you. I have always loved you and there is no one I'd rather live my life with, but I'm curious honey. I was a virgin when we married and you were the only man I'd ever known until a month ago. Troy and Mack showed me that there is so much out there that is different and I want to experience some of it. Tonight at cards when I tell Lisa that I'm not seeing Mack anymore she is going to want to fix me up with someone else and that's the problem baby. I want her to set me up with another guy, but I just can't do it behind your back anymore. The first time with Troy was an accident. It wasn't intentional - it just happened - but it was so unique an experience that I let it continue. With Mack I knew it was wrong, but I went ahead and did it anyway and I've felt nothing but guilt since. I don't want to feel guilty and I don't want to lose your love, but I do want to have a few more experiences."

Lorrie fell silent as I sat there and looked at her in total disbelief. "You are asking my permission to let you be a round heeled slut? My God Lorrie, didn't our marriage mean anything to you?"

"My marriage means everything to me John and you do too. That's why I'm asking - why I'm confessing. I love you and I'm hoping that you love me enough to overlook Troy and Mack and then I'm asking you to trust me. To let me have what I want and trust me to come home to you and to love you as much as I always have. Please John, all I'm asking is that you let me go out and sow a few wild oats. You go sow a few of your own if you want to. The only thing that is important is that we come back home to each other."

"I'm sorry that I'm such an old fashioned kind of guy. When I said my marriage vows I meant them - every word - and they didn't allow for sowing wild oats. You are asking me to let you go out and fuck other men and I'm not even sure that I can forgive you for the ones you have already fucked. And if that's not bad enough, what about the damage you may have already done? Troy "just happened" but did he happen to use a condom? He sounds promiscuous as hell, did he give you something that you in turn passed on to me? What about Mack? You say he likes to butt fuck and isn't that one of the biggest ways that AIDS gets spread? Did he use a condom? Did you even stop to consider that every one that Lisa sets you up with she has already sampled and haven't you already told me that she is having a ball fucking everything in pants? Just how many sexually transmitted diseases has she picked up and passed on. You're fucking with my life here Lorrie and I'm not fucking happy about it. I can't stop you from going out and fucking around if that's what you want to do, but it damned sure isn't going to be with my blessing. And if you do go out and do it I would just as soon that you don't bother coming home."

Lorrie just stared at me for several seconds and then she said, "I told you that I loved you. Do you really think that I didn't think of that? Even though my affair with Troy was a spur of the moment I still insisted that he use protection. Fortunately he loves to fuck women and he knows that if he picked up a disease and gave it to someone the word would go out and he'd be cut off, big cock or not so he always had rubbers handy. I didn't know how Mack would be so I made damn sure I had my own supply. I did not put you at risk and I would never put you at risk and I'm sorry that you have such a low opinion of me that you would think that I would."

She got up and left the table without saying another word. That night when we went to bed I reached out to touch her and she pulled away from me. For a minute I was angry and then suddenly I was laughing. I laughed so hard that I had to get out of bed. I went down to the living room and turned on the TV and started channel hopping. Five minutes later Lorrie came down, "What was that all about?"

"Think about it. I find out you are a cheating whore, I get angry about it, you get angry that I got angry and then when we are in bed I reach out to touch you and you pull away from me. It's just too fucking funny for words."

She stood there looking at me for several moments and then, "Yes, I guess it is" and then she sat down next to me on the couch. After maybe a minute she cuddled up to me and maybe two minutes after that her hand worked its way into my pajamas and she started stroking my cock. It responded and just before she took me in her mouth she said, "I'm sorry baby, I didn't mean to upset you. I do love you and I hope you know that."

Call me weak, call me pussy whipped, but I do love Lorrie and I know that she does love me so after a week of the two of us avoiding the subject and three weeks of talking about it I finally told Lorrie that she could satisfy her curiosity. And she did - in spades! She and Lisa would go out together after their card night, meet some men and then Lorrie would rush home and tell me what was different about the man she had just been with. At first I was a little put off by hearing Lorrie give me a blow by blow account of her evening with another man, but she was so animated and excited that it was infectious. I began to get a little turned on by the tales and soon they were leading to some spirited romps in the bedroom. Lorrie began asking me if I thought I might like to watch her with a man one night, "You get turned on when I tell you about it, maybe you would be even more turned on if you watched."

"Yes, and I might get so turned off that I would have to put an end to it."

For the next three months Lorrie screwed a new man every Thursday night. She had decided that having a two or three week affair, limiting herself to just one man for the period, could lead to emotional involvement and she didn't want that. Besides, a new man every week gave her a wider sample for her curiosity.

"I'm going to give it up one of these days and go back to being a good little wife. I need to see as much as I can until then."

Then came the night I got a phone call. It was Lorrie and she seemed to be a little out of breath, "I'm going to be real late tonight honey. Don't wait up. I'll tell you all about it in the morning." Lorrie wasn't home when I got up the next morning, but she did call me and tell me not to worry just before I left for work. "Take vitamins today sweetie, you will need them tonight." She wasn't wrong. The story she told me that night when I came home kept us in the bedroom for the entire weekend.

It hadn't been planned. One of the girls from Thursday night's card group was getting married and the other girls threw her a surprise bridal shower. There were a lot of gag gifts and some nice ones, but the centerpiece of the evening was the stripper that Lisa had hired to drop by. The stripper was a tall, well-built black man and he had knocked on the door dressed as a policeman who was investigating an excessive noise complaint. Then the music started and the clothes began coming off. Lisa had Marie sit in a chair in the middle of the room and the dancer took it all off in front of her. Then the girls got raunchy and started after Marie to reach out and touch the naked cock that was bouncing around only inches from her face, but Marie shut her eyes and turned her face away. The steam began to run out of the party and Lisa decided that she needed to crank it back up a notch.

"Let Lorrie show you how to do it," but Lorrie shook her head no. Then the other girls started stomping their feet and clapping their hands while crying out Lorrie, Lorrie, Lorrie." Still she hesitated. She had never had anything to do with blacks before and while she was curious she really didn't want to behave like a slut in front of her friends. As far as she knew only Lisa knew what a slut she had been being. But the girls kept up the chant and then Lisa said "I dare you" and Lorrie decided to go for it. She went down to her knees and the dancer moved over to her and waved his cock in her face and Lorrie opened her mouth and the stripper pushed his cock in. She sucked on it for several minutes while all the girls cheered her on and the stripper grabbed the back of her head and came in her mouth. She swallowed most of it, but some escaped her mouth and dribbled down her chin. Several of the girls came over to her and surprised her by taking some of the cum off her chin with their fingers and tasting it. Two of them said they wished they had her nerve and that they wished they would have done it. That made Lorrie feel better knowing that she was not going to be looked at as a slut by her peers.

After the dancer had dressed and was getting ready to leave he asked Lorrie if she would like to go to his apartment with him and finish what they had started. Lorrie told him no; that she and Lisa had to meet some people. The dancer (Derek) told her that he thought Lisa would love to meet his roommate and then Lisa had said, "Let's do it Lorrie, it will be fun." The girls followed Derek to his apartment where they were introduced to Jason and then they got down to it. Derek fucked Lorrie twice and then he said he would like a taste of Lisa and he and Jason switched partners. At some point, and Lorrie couldn't pinpoint when, either Jason or Derek had gone to a phone and put out the word that they had two cock loving white sluts that seemed to love black meat. When Lorrie had come home at ten in the morning she had trouble walking her pussy was so sore. She wasn't sure how many black men had shown up, but twenty-one of them had fucked her, several more that once, before she and Lisa said they had to leave. She told me that she had loved every second of it but didn't ever want to do it again.

But she did do it again. She became a regular visitor to Derek and Jason's apartment and they were always more than happy to invite their friends over while she was there. Lorrie pretty much fucks blacks exclusively now and she even goes out on dates with Derek or Jason on nights other than Thursday. I mean regular dates like dinner and a movie. They come to the house and pick her up while I hide in the back of the house and several times when they brought her home they fucked her in the driveway. She keeps after me to let her bring them in so I can hide in the closet and watch, but I'm nowhere near ready for that yet. I began to get concerned about Lorrie's fixation on blacks, but Lorrie told me not to worry. "They aren't super studs baby and they don't have huge cocks that I just have to have. It's just that I'm really getting off on the black/white taboo thing. I get a charge out of going out in public with them and having all of the uptight assholes look down their nose at me. I look back at them and give them a "Yes, he is going to fuck me tonight and you aren't" smile. It's a blast baby."

Lorrie keeps asking me if I've sown any wild oats and would I like her to bring Lisa home with her one night and I kept telling her it was no to both. And it was no until last night. Lorrie's younger sister Kelly and I are pretty close. She has always been more of a really good friend to me than a sister-in-law. About two months ago Kelly came to me in tears. She had just found out what her sister was doing.

"I don't know how she can do this to you. You have treated her like a queen all these years and then she goes and betrays you like this."

And then she filled me in on what Lorrie had done the night before. From then on, not knowing that I already knew, Kelly would come to me with "The Latest Outrage" that Lorrie had perpetrated on me and I would hang my head and say something stupid like, "Oh woe is me, whatever shall I do?" Kelly would rush to me, throw herself in my arms and try to comfort me. Then she would tell me that I needed to find some backbone, "You need to throw her worthless ass out John. You are too nice a guy to let her screw over you like this."

I suppose I could have told her what was going on, but the truth of the matter is that I rather liked Kelly throwing herself in my arms. At 4'9" and 110 pounds and with a nice rack (34C) Kelly was one very sexy armful and I could never figure out why her idiot husband had left her for some blonde bimbo. So I played the befuddled and betrayed husband to her outraged sister of the slutty wife. I won't say that I had never ever given any thought to bedding Kelly, but I knew I would never do it because of the fact she was Lorrie's sister. But I had never given any thought to what Kelly might want or do.

It was a Thursday night and Lorrie had already gone to her card party. The doorbell rang and when I answered it Kelly walked in. She didn't say a word, just walked straight past me and went down the hall to my bedroom. When she hadn't come back in five minutes I went to see what she was doing. I found her on my bed. She was naked except for thigh highs and high heels and when I walked into the room she said, "If you aren't going to do anything about that whore you are married to you should at least have some fun yourself. Do you like my pussy? I shaved it just for you."

She was my wife's sister so technically it wasn't incest, but still, she was Lorrie's sister. How Lorrie was going to feel about it I didn't know, but I did know that there wasn't any way that I was going to pass up what was lying spread out on the bed in front of me. It would be an interesting conversation when Lorrie got home and I told her that I'd finally had some fun of my own. As I undressed I wondered just how open minded Lorrie really was. I'd certainly know by morning.

The End

Carla's Revenge

I've found out that my wife is cheating on me and so far she and Josh don't know that I know. Josh by the way is – or was – my best friend. I know, I know, it is a cliché, but clichés get to be clichés because they happen so often.

I had no idea of how I was going to handle it. The thing was that I couldn't understand why he was fucking my wife. Don't get me wrong here; my wife is definitely a hottie. She is in her mid-thirties and even after three kids she looks hot as hell in a bikini, but his wife Carla is just as hot if not hotter. She was fairly tall at five foot seven, has red hair that hangs down to the middle of her back and has green eyes that seem to be able to look deep into your soul. I found out that she comes in at 36-23-34 and I won't deny that she turned me on.

I let things slide for a couple of weeks after finding out about Josh and Heather as I tried to make up my mind about what to do. I loved Heather and I wondered if there was some way to save our marriage. It didn't seem likely, but I couldn't know for sure until we talked. On Friday I made up my mind to confront her on Monday. Why the two day wait? Heather had gotten a call from a very sick friend who had needed some help and she had rushed off to help her.

I knew without a doubt that if I called Josh to ask him if he wanted to play golf on Saturday I'd get Carla and she would tell me that Josh wasn't there and was off doing something over the weekend. My parents had taken the kids up to their cabin on the lake for the weekend so no wife and no kids meant that I was going to spend a quiet weekend alone and it could very well be the last quiet weekend I would ever have.

On the way home I stopped and got a case of beer and I fully intended to see that all twenty-four bottles were empty by Sunday night. When I got home I put on a pair of shorts and a tee shirt and went into the kitchen. Dinner that night was going to be simple. I opened a package of hot dogs and put them in a pan to boil, chopped up an onion and got a can of baked beans out of the pantry. I dumped the beans in a pot and put it on a burner and then opened my second beer.

I was digging through the fridge looking for the mustard when the doorbell rang. When I opened the door I found Carla standing there. She was wearing a tank top and it looked like she wasn't wearing a bra. She had on a pair of Daisy Dukes and a pair of flip flops on her feet. Her nipples were pushing hard at the tank top and I got instant major wood.

"You doing anything important?" she asked.

"Batching it. Working on dinner and drinking beer."

"Mind if I join you?"

"Not in the least. I could use the company," I said as I stepped aside and let her in. We walked to the kitchen and she sat down at the table. I knew she didn't drink beer so I opened a bottle of Merlot and I poured her a glass.

"Dinner is nothing fancy," I said. "Hot dogs and baked beans. Pretty simple stuff."

"I can do simple."

The hot dogs were boiling and the beans were bubbling so I turned off the heat and moved the pans to the cold side of the stove and got two plates from the cupboard. I handed Carla one and told her to help herself. She fixed herself two hot dogs and spooned some beans on her plate. We sat down to eat and I asked:

"What brings you over?"

"You have any idea where Heather is?"

"She went to help a sick friend."

"I wonder when it happened?"

"When what happened?"

"When Josh got sick. He looked pretty damned healthy to me when he left the house. You do know that Josh is fucking Heather right? And that right now they are in room 130 at the Arrowhead Lodge?"

"I didn't know that they were at the Arrowhead, but I've known for a couple of weeks now that she has been cheating on me. How did you find out?"

"I found part of a condom wrapper in his pants pocket when I was doing the laundry. He doesn't use them with me because we have been trying to get me pregnant. I decided not to have his baby if he was cheating on me. I didn't want to end up as a single mother if there was going to be a divorce so I used some of the inheritance from my dad to put a private detective on him. They get together for long lunches and when he calls and tells me that he is working late he is usually working on Heather. How did you find out?"

"I was in the basement working on a bookcase I'm making. The phone rang and I picked up the basement extension. Heather must have picked up the upstairs phone a second or so ahead of me and I heard her say the word "lover" just as I put the phone to my ear so I quietly listened while Josh told her they would have to skip their usual long lunch at the Marriott because on an important meeting he had to go to. I got to listen to her tell him that she would miss his cock and that he was going to have to work hard to make it up to her the next time."

"You haven't done anything about it?"

"I haven't been able to make up my mind as to what to do. I did decide this afternoon to confront her when she gets home and see where it goes from there. What are you going to do?"

"Hopefully I'll be doing it in a few minutes."

I gave her what must have seemed to her like a confused look and said, "Do what?"

She got up and came over and sat down on my lap. "I've seen the way you look at me and I know damned well that if we weren't married you would have been after me. We might both still be married, but we don't owe Josh and Heather any more fidelity that they have given us."

She hugged me and her hand slid up my leg, under my shorts and to the leg band of my briefs. I shifted to get a little more comfortable and her hand went under my briefs and touched my cock. I looked at her in amazement and she leaned into me and her lips met mine. She slipped her tongue into my mouth and her hand gripped my hard cock. No silly fool me I kissed her back and swapped tongues with her. She broke the kiss and said:

"I'm going for the ultimate in revenge. Even though we decided to have a baby I've managed to come up with excuses not to have sex during my fertile times and to be on the safe side I went to my doctor and was fitted for a diaphragm. How bad do you want revenge on Josh?"

"Why do you ask that?"

"It is my ultimate revenge. I'm at my most fertile right now and my diaphragm is in my purse."

"You mea…"

"That is exactly what I mean."

Carla was right. It would be the ultimate revenge to have Josh raising my kid thinking that it was his. I smiled and moved a hand up under Carla's tank top and discovered that I had been right when I guessed that she was braless and I felt her right nipple. It was as hard as a pencil eraser and when I pulled on it Carla moaned. Her mouth fastened on mine and I sent my other hand under her Daisy Duke's and discovered that she was not only braless, but she wasn't wearing any panties.

I slowly worked a finger into her wet pussy and she moaned and whispered, "Oh yes" as I worked my finger. I broke the kiss and said:

"On Heather's side of the bed. That's where I want you; on Heather's side of the bed."

She got off my lap and said, "Let's go."

We both hurriedly stripped when we got to the bedroom and Carla naked was spectacular and she had something that I had never seen before except in men's magazines – she was completely shaved! I have already mentioned that Heather was a hottie, but why Josh was fucking my wife when he had a woman like Carla made absolutely no sense to me. Carla was apparently thinking along the same lines. She was looking at my naked body with a puzzled look on her face and when I asked her what she was thinking she said:

"I just don't understand it. Your cock is both longer and thicker than Josh's so why in the world would Heather want to fuck my husband when she has you and that cock at home and ready to go. Makes no sense to me."

"Doesn't matter. You are here now and for the time being those other two people don't even exist."

"You are so right. Take me to bed and do it now."

I pointed at Heather's side of the bed and she smiled and said, "You do me on Heather's side of the bed and then we can go to my place and I'll do you on Josh's side of the bed."

"Deal." I said as she laid back on the bed and spread her legs. I moved between them and she lifted her legs and told me to fuck her and fuck her hard.

"Can't do it. Not until I've had a taste."

I put my mouth on that hairless pussy and lapped at it until Carla cried out "Enough! Fuck me."

I moved up and pushed forward and my cock spread her lips slid into her hot wet hole.

"Oh yessss" she hissed, "Fill me lover; fill me and fuck me hard."

I did what the lady asked. I was grunting and she was moaning as we went after each other like two animals in heat. The sound of my balls slapping her ass as I drove into bounced off the walls of the room. She begged me not to stop and to keep fucking her forever. Her words were driving me crazy with lust and I wanted to do what she wanted me to do. I did want to keep fucking her forever. I pounded and pounded and pounded. I needed to get her off before I got mine. I was close, damned close and luckily Carla started cumming and I felt her pussy clamp down on my cock and I couldn't hold it back any longer. I came and pumped what felt like a gallon of cum into her fertile womb.

Both of us were sweaty and gasping for breath when I pulled out of her and fell to the bed beside her. Carla rolled up on an elbow and looked down at me.

"I can't believe this. I just can't believe this. Heather can have this and she wants my husband?"

Her hand reached for my wet cock and she started to fondle it. My cock twitched and Carla said:

"Good boy. Showing signs of life and that's a good thing 'cause we ain't even close to being done yet lover. I've got two more holes that you have to claim by cumming in them. We have the rest of tonight, all of tomorrow and part of Sunday and when I'm through with you, you won't give a rat's ass if Heather ever comes home."

She moved down and started licking my cock and then her mouth captured it and she began to work on it. A cock that had been limp only minutes before quickly became iron bar hard. She pulled her mouth of off of me and then she moved up and mounted me. "My turn to ride," she said as she started fucking me cowgirl style.

Carla rode me to the point where I just had to get off and I rolled her over on her back and fucked her hard until we both climaxed and as we rested she said:

"You aren't going to make me go home tonight are you?"

"Silly girl" I said as I pulled her to me. We fell asleep wrapped around each other.

***

I woke before Carla did in the morning and as I lay there looking at her I couldn't help but think that what I had done with Josh's wife didn't make me any better than Heather. Granted that I could rationalize it by saying that Heather cheated on me and that released me from my vows. She did so I could right? What's good for the goose is good for the gander right? Turn about is fair play right? But for me the bottom line was that I had cheated on my marriage. I couldn't claim the high ground when I confronted Heather. True, she didn't know that I had done it, but I knew.

I hadn't noticed that Carla was awake until she said, "You look deep in thought. What are you thinking?"

I told her and she said, "I made the same promises you did when I married Josh so I guess that makes me a cheater also, but I don't look at it that way. Josh made the same vows as I did and then he broke them. To me that meant we had a contract and if we were dealing in law, if I remember rightly from my Business Law classes, Josh would be in breach of contract and the contract could be declared null and void. I know marriages aren't handled that way, but it doesn't change the fact that Josh and I had a contract and he broke that contract with me That means, at least to me, that I no longer have to honor that contract unless I so choose. You need to look at your marriage the same way. You aren't cheating lover; you are only doing what her breach of her contract with you has freed you up to do. Enough of this stuff. Take me out and feed me and then we need to go to my place and rededicate Josh's side of the bed and work on getting me pregnant."

Her hand started moving down my body and by the time she reached my groin area I was already starting to rise and then we were off and running. If she wasn't pregnant by the time we fell asleep at her place it wasn't because we didn't try hard enough. I don't think that the last two times we made love did any good because I don't believe much more than dust came out of the end of my cock.

In the morning she asked me what time the kids would be home and I told her around six. She fed me steak and eggs for breakfast saying that I'd need my energy if I was going to do her any good that day.

We called it quits around four so I could head home and be there in case my parents got there earlier than expected. Before I went home Carla asked me if I had made up my mind as to what I was going to do and I admitted that I hadn't.

"Are you a good enough actor to pretend that everything is fine?"

"I don't know. Why?"

"Because to my mind the best revenge is for us to keep doing what we spent the weekend doing. I want to keep on doing it until I'm pregnant. Also you need to think about your kids. A divorce will cut you off from them because around here the courts always give custody to the mother. You would maybe get to see them every other weekend and that would only be if Heather wasn't pissed off enough at you to find some excuse that you couldn't have them that weekend. My advice would be to put up with the bitch. Life as usual except that you and I would be fucking up a storm every chance we could get."

"I don't know about that Carla. Sooner or later cheaters will get caught. If they catch us it reduces our chance to hold the high ground in any talks we have."

"They got caught because of stupid mistakes. You found out about Heather because the two of them were dumb enough to use the home phones to communicate. I found out because Josh was so sloppy that he brought the evidence home in his pants pocket. We won't take those kinds of chances. We will get a couple of Tracfones from Wal-Mart and use them to keep in touch and so that our spouses won't accidentally find them and wonder about them we will leave them in our desks at work. We will always know when they are getting together so we will get together at the same time."

"No, we won't be able to do that. If Heather calls and says she has to work late I'll have to babysit and if they are doing it on their lunch hours we won't be able to because I can only rarely take long lunches."

"You can sometimes work late can't you? When you do she will have to be home to watch the kids. I play cards with some sorority sisters from college every Wednesday night and I sometimes stop for drinks after work with the people I work with and Josh is used to that. Another thing we can do is put a tap on our phone lines so we will know what they are talking about. Are you game?"

"You've thought it all out haven't you?"

"Maybe I've missed something, but with both of us working together I think we can cover all the bases."

"You are sure you want to do this?"

"Absolutely sure. Like I told you in the beginning I want revenge on Josh. I gave him everything I have and he stabs me in the back. I spoil that son of a bitch rotten and fuck his eyes out three and four times a week and he cheats on me? No damned way I'm going to let it slide. My idea of the perfect revenge is to let him raise another man's kid and what could be sweeter than having the husband of the woman he is cheating with being that father of that child."

"I can see the need for revenge and I guess I can get behind seeing that asshole raise my kid, but I'm not all that sure that I can pull off pretending to be a loving husband to a wife who is cheating on me."

"You have incentive lover."

"I do?"

"Over the last forty-eight hours you seemed to love the hell out of what I gave you. You can have as much of it as you want, any time you want and for as long as you want."

"You do know that's a damned hard offer to refuse."

"I would certainly hope so and there is more. Josh wants two kids, a boy and a girl and I am going to want the both of them to have the same daddy. It could be even better than that. What if I get the first two and they are both girls? I know he is going to want a son. You up to keeping on trying?"

"I am as long as we don't get caught."

"We will just have to make sure that that doesn't happen. Oh, and one last thing. Can you act natural around Josh?"

"It will be hard not to smirk knowing that I'm going to be trying my best to give him a kid to raise, but I think that I'll be able to handle it."

"I think Tuesday will be my next night to stop after work with the girls."

"What a coincidence. I'll be working late on Tuesday."

***

My folks dropped the kids off at six-thirty and told me that they hadn't eaten yet so I took them out to Mickey Ds and wasn't the least bit surprised when they told me that they wanted Happy Meals. After we ate we went home and found Heather there and she asked where we had been and when I told her she said in a snippy tone:

"Why didn't you call me and see if I wanted to go to dinner with you?"

"You didn't tell me when you would be back and you didn't call my cell and tell me you were back," I answered in the same snippy tone.

She gave me a nasty look and then went to say hi to the kids. While Heather put the kids to bed I went on line and did a search. I found out how to tap a phone line using a voice activated tape recorder and decided to buy one or two on my way home from work the next day. I'd buy two so I could put a tap on not only my line, but one on Josh's line also. I'd have to call Carla and set it up.

I noticed that Heather didn't shower before coming to bed. She might have showered before coming home, but then again maybe she didn't and I had no intentions of taking sloppy seconds. I probably had in the past, but I didn't know it then. When Heather made overtires I pleaded an upset stomach and told her maybe the next day.

Monday at three-twenty my secretary told me that there was a Mrs. Carla Marvis who would like to see me and I told Shelly to send Carla in. Carla came in and closed the door behind her and came over to me and kissed me.

"Too bad you have a secretary sitting right outside your door. If she wasn't there I'd lock the door and you could do me right here on your desk."

'If you can kill ten minutes she goes home at three-thirty."

"Oh wow! I was just kidding, but I can easily kill ten minutes."

She opened her purse and took out a cell phone and handed it to me and told me that she had already programmed her number into it.

"The plan for tomorrow is that at lunch time I'm going to run over to the Marriott and get a room. I picked the Marriott because you have to go inside and go down a hall to get to the rooms. No outside doors that someone could see us go into. I'll call you and give you the room number. I'll get off work at four-thirty and go right to the room. When you get there, go into the bar and have a drink and if anyone there knows you and sees you they will think that you just stopped in for a drink on the way home. After your drink you come to the room where I will be naked and waiting. Okay?"

"Sounds like a plan to me. On the way home I'm picking up what we need to tap our phones. When would be a good time for me to come over and do it?"

"It is already done. I went online and found out how to do it and I already had a recorder that I could use."

At that point Shelly stuck her head in the door and said, "I'm leaving Mr. B and I'll see you in the morning."

When the door closed Carla got up to lock the door and when she turned back to me I already had my pants and briefs off and was clearing the desk. Carla laughed and said:

"Eager? I like that in a man," she said as she lifted her skirt and took off her panties.

It was a quick no frills fuck and we both got off and as Carla was putting her panties back on she said:

"That will hold me till tomorrow, but you had better come to the room prepared for a long and energetic evening. Maybe you should load up on vitamins."

I debated washing my cock before I went home. If I fucked Heather that night it would be a kick to do it with Carla's juices – probably dried by then – still on my cock, but Heather usually started me out with oral and she might just question the taste. Better safe than sorry I thought and headed for the men's room to clean up.

I stopped at Radio Shack on the way home and bought two recorders and six extra tapes. I got the second recorder so I could listen to the tapes in my office. I would save any tape that had something on it from the two lovers against the day I would be telling a judge why I wanted a divorce.

Heather had dinner ready when I got home and she had wine out which was a good sign that she was in an amorous mood and I wondered at that. She had spent the weekend fucking her lover and she comes home wanting more? Was she turning into a nymphomaniac or did she just get off on doing her clueless (or so she thought) husband after being with her lover. Maybe someday I'd find out the answer to that one.

Sex was always good with Heather and she liked to do it all. She gave pretty good head – not as good as Carla – and she liked anal. If Carla had been honest and not just playing to my ego when she said I was bigger than Josh I had to wonder what he had that Heather thought that I was lacking. Another question that I might someday get an answer to.

When dinner was over and the kids were parked in front of the electronic babysitter and we were doing the dishes Heather said:

"You do know that you have your work cut out for you tonight right?"

"Oh?" And why's that?"

"You have to make up for last night."

"I'll do my best."

"Your best is always spectacular my love."

I wanted to say, "Then why are you fucking Josh" but I kept my mouth shut.

While Heather read to the kids I went down into the basement, found where the phone line came into the house and put a tap on the phone. Heather didn't leave for work until an hour after I did and I guessed that is when she and Josh would do most of their talking. I could be wrong about that. Heather had a cell phone and of course they could possibly talk on her work phone while she was at work. I was gambling that the call I'd overheard was a sign that they talked when she was at home.

We went three times that night which was a rare event for us. We had sex three or four times a week, but usually only once although on occasion we did go twice. One more thing to wonder about. The warning bell went off just after we had finished our third time. We were lying next to each other when Heather said:

"Have you given any thought to us having another child?"

"Not really," I said as I thought especially not Josh's. "In fact I have been flirting with the idea of getting a vasectomy so you could give up birth control pills and we could still be safe."

"Why wouldn't you want another?"

"We had Mike and Anna so soon after our wedding that we never had a chance to go places and do things. As it sits now we will still be young enough to do some things when Mike and Anna strike out on their own. More kids would prevent that. Besides, right now we need the income from your job. We would be pinched if you had to leave work because of a pregnancy."

In my mind I was thinking some real bad thoughts. Heather and Carla talked and I'm sure that Heather knew that Carla and Josh had decided to try and have a child. Did Heather want to get Josh's first child before Carla could get it? Was there something that Heather had against Carla or was it just Heather trying to stake a claim to her lover? Either way it didn't make me think I could follow through on Carla's plan. In my mind I was going to have to dump Heather pretty damned soon.

Then I had a very, very bad thought. Were Mike and Anna even mine? I was going to have to find out. I fell into a very disturbed sleep.

***

The next afternoon after an exhausting session in room 202 of the downtown Marriott, I voiced my concerns to Carla.

"I can't even make a wild guess as to what you should do," Carla said. "Confront her about Josh now before he can get her pregnant? Of course she could already be pregnant and is getting ready to drop it on you. I know what I'd do, but I'm not a man and I'm not you."

"What would you do?"

"I'd just tell her that I want no more kids so to be safe I would start wearing a condom until I could get a vasectomy. If she does come up pregnant that is when I would have the confrontation. I'd say that I guess we need a DNA test to see if it was mine or Josh's. That should rock her back on her heels."

"If I get a vasectomy it will blow our revenge plan."

"Just don't get it until you get me pregnant. It will be a shame because I do so want all my kids to have the same father. We might get lucky. Maybe Heather was only sounding you out on having another and you saying you didn't want another will make her drop it. We just won't ever know unless she comes up to you and says that the rabbit died."

She looked at her watch and said, "We have time for a couple more chances for you to make me a mommy."

I stopped on the way home and got a bunch of condoms and that night when Heather wanted sex I got one of the condoms out and started to put it on.

"What's that for?"

"I've decided to use them until I can get a vasectomy. I really don't want any more kids."

"Well take it off. I hate the feel of those things. I'll stay on the pill and use spermicides until I can get fitted for a diaphragm. That should keep us plenty safe."

"Hated the feel of them?" I thought as I finished rolling it on. Heather was a virgin when we got married and I had never used a rubber with her. When did she learn that she didn't like the feel of them? And with who? Whatever! It just reinforced my decision to find out about the paternity of my two children. Then I remembered that it was because of Josh using rubbers when he fucked Heather that had clued Carla into the fact that Josh was cheating on her. I was still going to get the tests done.

I finished rolling it on and said, "Unless you already have the spermicide I'll use the raincoats that I bought today."

"I don't, but I'll get some tomorrow and make a doctor's appointment for the diaphragm. I don't want you getting a vasectomy. I want to keep the option open in case you ever change your mind."

I left the rubber on, got on the bed and went down on her. When she reached the point where she grabbed my head and tried to pull it inside her I pulled away from her and then slid my cock into her. She came quickly and then I took my time bringing her to another climax before picking up the pace and getting my nut. I held myself in her until I was soft and then I pulled out, removed the cover and went into the bathroom to dispose of it. When I got back to the bed Heather was lying on her side asleep.

I figured that it was a good time to head down to the basement and check the recorder. A couple of junk calls and then:

"Hello?"

"Good morning sweetie. Miss me?"

"Of course I do."

"We still on for lunch today?"

"Yes, but I think our lunch meetings are about over unless we can find some place where it won't cost so much. Those motel rooms are killing my family budget. I can't keep pulling from it. Sooner or later I won't have enough in it to feed my family and I damned sure don't want Bob asking why."

"I'll try to come up with something. Wednesday night is the cunt's card night. You figured out a way to get out of the house yet?"

"Not yet, but I'm working on it."

"I'll cross my fingers. I need more of you than I get on a forty-five minute lunch break."

"Me too lover."

"Talk to you tomorrow?"

"Of course."

"Till then."

"Bye baby."

I almost puked when I realized that I had eaten Heather's pussy after she had let Josh use it that afternoon, but I managed not to. I found it interesting that the whore was not only cheating on me, but she had to pay for the room to do it in. I wondered how Carla would take it when she heard that she was a "cunt" according to her hubby. The only thing I knew for sure as I climbed the steps up out of the basement is that Heather was not going to be able to get out of the house on Wednesday night.

Tuesday when I got to work I took the Tracfone out of my desk drawer and called Carla and when she answered I said:

"Good morning cunt."

"What? Who the hell is this?"

"You have forgotten the voice of the father to be of your children already? And besides, who else has this number?"

"Bob? What are you doing calling me a cunt?"

"Give a listen to this" I said as I held the recorder up to the phone and hit play. After "The cunt's card night" had played I said, "See? On good authority I have it that you are a cunt. A husband knows these things about his wife right?"

"When the time comes I'll kill the fucking asshole."

I played the rest of the tape for her since she obviously hadn't checked the recorder that she had put on her home line and after she listened to it she asked me what I was going to do.

"I think I'll have to work late Wednesday, but I won't let her know until it is almost time for her to get off work. Hopefully it will be too short a notice for her to line up a baby sitter. Did you catch the part where Heather says she is paying for the room they cheat in?"

"Doesn't surprise me. Josh has always been cheap. I guess if you are going to work late I'll skip my card night and we can get together."

"I'll call you tomorrow and set it up"

Wednesday over breakfast Heather did ask me if I had plans for the evening and I told her no and asked why she wanted to know.

"The girls from work have been talking about stopping after work to have a couple of drinks and socialize away from work. I can't do it unless you are here to watch the kids."

"Shouldn't be a problem."

I kissed her and headed off for work. I stopped off at the Marriott and got a room and when I got to work I called Carla and gave her the room number. Heather gets off work at five so at four-forty I called her and told her that I had to work late.

"There are some problems with the Henderson contract and they have to be taken care of before Nathan goes to his meeting with them in the morning. Sorry for such short notice, but I really can't get out of it. I may be really late so don't wait up for me. Love you. Bye."

I spent an exhausting time in room 333 and Heather was asleep when I got home. If she had been up and had wanted to play I'm not sure that I could have gotten it up for her.

***

For the next five weeks Carla and I were able to get together on the average of twice a week and it helped to always know ahead of time by way of the phone taps what Josh and Heather were up to. It was during that fifth week that Carla said:

"Congratulations daddy. How about fucking the eyes out of the mother of your child?"

"How does Josh feel about it?"

"He doesn't know yet. I needed to tell the baby's father first. Then I can tell Josh."

"You know," I said, "The one thing we haven't done that they have is go off for a weekend together. I think we owe it to ourselves to have one to celebrate your pregnancy. We just need to do it without the two of them putting two and two together and coming up with the right answer."

"Funny that you should bring that up at this exact time. Josh has to fly to San Diego to handle some detail or other with his father's estate. He is going over this weekend so he can visit with some relatives before going to see the attorney on Monday. If you can come up with a way to get out for the weekend we can go someplace and neither one would have any reason to think about it.

"I think I can do it."

I got off the bed and got my cell phone and called my brother who lived in Akron. When I got him I asked him to call the house just after I left for work in the morning and to tell Heather that I need to come home for a family emergency of some type over the weekend. I told him

I'd call him later and clue him in as to what was going on. He said he would take care of it and we said goodbye.

I turned to Carla and said, "All that's left is to decide where we want to go."

The next morning Heather called me on my cell about five minutes after I left the house.

"You need to call Bill as soon as possible. There is a family emergency and he needs to talk with you."

"I'll call him as soon as you hang up."

I waited until I got to work and then called Bill.

"I told her that Brian (his son) needs a kidney transplant and I needed to see if you would be willing to donate a kidney and if so would you come back and be tested to see if you would be a good match. What's up?"

I explained the situation to him and he told me that I could count on him to help any time I needed it. I knew I could count on him because he hated cheating sluts. He was a single father because his wife had cheated on him. He had kicked her out and had ended up with the kids when Martha had died in an auto accident.

I called Carla and told her the set up and we made arrangements to take off for the weekend. I got on the phone and called the Arrowhead Lodge and was even able to reserve room 130. Only fitting I thought. At two I called Heather and told her that I was flying back to Akron.

"I'll stop by the house and pack a bag. My flight leaves at eight and I need to get there at least a half hour early to check in."

"I hate to sound selfish, but I do hope that you aren't a match. I need you to have all your parts to ensure we make it all the way to old age together."

"Damn Heather; the way you say that makes me think you might actually love me."

"There better not be any doubt in your mind about it buster. Not even a smidgen."

If you only knew what I thought as I said goodbye and hung up the phone.

When I got home Heather was waiting for me in what she called her "Fuck me" suit. Naked with 'come fuck me' pumps on. "Got time to give me something to hold me until you get back?"

Since I really didn't need to hurry to catch a non-existent flight I said that I had the time.

Heather was lying on the bed with my cum leaking out of her pussy and as I dressed she said:

"On the phone you almost sounded like you doubted that I love you."

"Just kidding babe. I know full well how much you love me."

You show me just how much every time you fuck Josh.

"I don't want you to ever doubt it lover. Not ever."

***

The weekend with Carla was exhausting. Make love and go to bed. Wake up in the morning, make love and then go to breakfast. Go back to the room and make love until lunch time. Eat and then go back to the room and make love. Go out and sit by the pool for a while and then go back to the room and make love. Go out to dinner, have a few drinks and dance a little and then go back to the room and make love. Repeat the next day and then once more when we woke up Monday morning. We promised each other that we would do it again and then headed home.

Heather was at work when I got home so I went to the basement and checked the recorder. The first call on Friday morning was Bill. A couple of minutes after she hung up on Bill she got a call from Josh.

"You figure out a way to get loose for the weekend? I'd love to spend a couple of uninterrupted days with you."

"No Josh; I haven't been able to think of a way and the truth of the matter is that I don't want to come up with a way."

"What's the matter? Why not?"

"The guilt over what I've been doing has finally caught up with me. I love Bob and he deserves better than to have a cheating wife. The next time we got together I was going to tell you that it was over. I need to devote myself to Bob."

"Oh come on Heather; you have been making love with me for almost a year. How could you do that if you love him as much as you say?"

"First off I need to correct something that you just said. I've never made love to you. I have fucked you, but never ever made love with you. The only man I make love to is Bob."

"Bullshit!"

"No Josh; not bullshit. I love the man and I try to show him that I love him every chance that I get."

"If you love him so much why have you been doing me?"

"The excitement of it. The thrill of doing something illicit and forbidden. It was a major turn on for me to go home and make love to Bob after I'd fucked you. It gave me some humongous orgasms."

"It turned you on to give him sloppy seconds? If that's the case why not keep on going?"

"I have never given him sloppy seconds. I was always clean when I made love to him."

"Bullshit Heather. You never showered before we left the motel rooms."

"I keep a travel bag at work and it has everything that I needed to douche with. Bob has never even come close to feeling even a small trace of you.' No Josh; I'm ending it before we get caught. I love Bob and I don't want to lose him. Just be happy that you managed to get me drunk and take advantage of me the first time."

"Maybe so, but you weren't drunk all the other times."

"Depends on what you mean by drunk. I was drunk on the thrill I got from making love to Bob after you had fucked me. I wanted to see if the thrill and excitement would be there if I did it sober so I let you do me a second time and it was and that is the only reason I kept on doing it. We've gotten away with it for a little over a year, but I've just woken up to the fact that the feeling I get going to Bob after being with you isn't worth what it would cost me if we got caught and I lost Bob. Have fun in California Josh and when you get home don't call me. Bye."

Interesting I thought as I pulled the tape and inserted a fresh one.

I unpacked and headed to work. Around eleven I called Carla and when I said "Hi" she said, "Miss me all ready?"

"You know it sexy. I've got something I want you to hear."

"If it is Friday's phone conversation I've already heard it."

"What do you think?"

"It sounds like she got her head out of her ass and realized that she could lose you. What are you going to do?"

"I'd already made up my mind to hang in there until the kids turned eighteen and I can't see anything that would make me change my mind. If she meant what she said to Josh it will make it easier to stick it out, but the trust is gone. Even if she does break it off with Josh and they never get together again how do I know that somewhere down the line she won't start missing the thrill and excitement of cheating and hook up with some new guy?"

"You could always hit her with "If you are really through with Josh maybe we can move on, but you get no second chance."

"No I couldn't. That would give up the information that I have a tap on the phone and like I said, the trust is gone. I'm going to need a way to keep track of what she is up to. Besides, she knows me and she would know that if I knew I would have shared it with you. She might tell that to Josh and that might get him to thinking and we don't want that."

"Is that your roundabout way of saying that we are going to keep on going?"

"You heard the tape. They've gotten away with it for a little over a year and you and I have only been at it for a couple of months. They owe us another ten or twelve months and then of course there are the penalties and interest that could make it even longer."

"I'd like that."

Epilogue

Carla and I continued to see each other on the average of twice a week until her seventh month. She wanted to keep going, but she was so big with the babies that I didn't think I could make love to her without hurting her. That's right – babies. The ultrasound showed that Carla was going to have twins. She gave birth to two beautiful little girls.

True to her prediction Josh wanted a son so two years after the birth of the twins I got her pregnant again and this time the ultrasound said it was a boy. We made love until her eighth month and then we called it quits. We both felt that we had gotten away with it long enough and to get caught at that point would turn Carla into a single mom with three kids to raise and neither of us wanted that. As Carla put it on our last time together:

"The object was to get revenge on the cheating bastard by giving him another man's kids to raise. I need to stay married to him for that to happen."

Josh received a promotion that required him to move and I haven't seen or talked to Carla since they moved however I do think of her often and fondly.

It has been six years now and as far as I know – at least according to the telephone tap – Heather hasn't hooked up with anyone else, but then she and Josh had gotten away with what they were doing for over a year before I found out about them and I hadn't a clue. She could have possibly gotten smart enough to stop using the home phone, but I keep a close eye on her and so far I haven't seen anything that would indicate that she is fooling around.

She has been doing her best to spoil me rotten and I have been rethinking my plan to bail out when the kids hit eighteen and that will be four more years for Mike and five more for Anna.

I'll just have to wait and see.

The End

Alice At The Office

My husband, while he was still my boyfriend, worked for a long time to convince me that my legs were great and that I needed to show them off properly. He was the one who talked me into wearing high heels, nylons, garter belts, crotchless pantyhose and short skirts so I guess he can be considered responsible for the story I'm about to relate.

***

I'd just been laid off and I was looking for a new job. A small sales firm had an ad in the paper for a secretary/receptionist and while the pay offered was lower than what I was looking for the job did have the advantage of only being a five-minute walk from where I lived. The money I would save on downtown parking and other transportation costs made it worth looking into.

I applied and was called in for an interview. I arrived for my interview wearing a nice summer print that came down to just below the knee and white pumps with a three-inch heel. The interview was one of the strangest that I've ever had. The first question that George, the owner, asked me was not about my typing skills, my familiarity with the phone system, my spelling or my ability to take dictation, but "How would you feel about being a sex object for eight hours a day?"

Apparently the look on my face answered that question and also told him that I was getting ready to stand up and go storming out of the place so he hastened to explain. The people who called on him during the course of the business day sometimes had to wait a considerable amount of time before he could see them. The longer the wait the more agitated the person would become. George said that he had discovered that the way to diffuse the situation was place an attractive receptionist, one who would not mind the attention she would draw, in the outer office. In fact, he said, the best receptionist's for his purposes where the ones who invited appreciative glances.

I must have softened my expression some because George smiled at me and said that he couldn't help but notice that I had great legs and looked very sexy in high heels. He said if I wore heels all the time I would be perfect for the job since the receptionist's desk was open front and my legs would always be on display. I told George that I had no problem with being admired, but I was not about to put myself in a position where I would constantly be fighting off unwanted advances. George assured me that none of his girls had ever had that problem. All I had to do, he said, was look good for the people waiting while I was performing my other duties.

"Just keep their attention so they won't think about being kept waiting."

I did have to admit that the job did appeal to the exhibitionist in me, but I was hesitant and I told George that I would like some time to consider. He told me that he could give until noon the next day, but that he considered me perfect for the position and he would up the salary by $250 a month if I would take the job.

To shorten the story, I took the job and everything was just as George said it would be. I sat at the desk and displayed a lot of leg and the callers appeared to be enjoying every bit of it. I took to wearing shorter skirts and opening my legs wider as I sat at the desk. I made it a habit to do a lot of filing in the bottom drawer of the filing cabinet (even though I did need to go back later and re-file some of it) bending at the waist so the skirt would ride up and show some panty. Cock teasing and I knew it, but hey, that's what I was being paid for, right?

Since I live close to work I usually walked if the weather was nice and on those days I would carry my heels in a bag and change when I got to work. This got to be a pain so I started leaving the shoes that I wore the most often at work. One evening, about three months ago, I left work to walk home and about three blocks from the office I remembered that I had left some personal papers in my center desk drawer. When I got back to the office I found two pair of my heels sitting in the middle of my desk which was strange because I had left them in the lower left hand drawer. As I bent over the desk I noticed that the light was still on in George's office and the door was partially open. I walked over to the door with the intention of asking George if he knew what was going on with my shoes, but as I got closer to the partially opened door I could see into the office and what I saw answered my question.

I could see George sitting in his chair with his trousers off, his cock out and erect, and he was stroking it with one of my white pumps while his nose was buried in its mate. I froze and tried to stay quiet while I watched him masturbate using my pumps. I must have stood there ten minutes while he ran the pump all over his cock and some of the things he did had to be painful, but he didn't seem to notice – or care. He finally put down the shoe he had buried his nose in and began to furiously stroke his cock and, just as the sperm shot out, he put the remaining shoe where it could catch all the cum, some into it and some on the toe. I carefully backed away and left the office.

I don't know why, but I felt like I had been violated and by the time I got home I had decided that I would go to work the next day, confront George and then quit. I told my husband about what happened and he had laughed and said I should give the poor guy a break. After all, who was he hurting? Was he causing anyone a problem? What did I have to gain by quitting? I decided that my husband was right. George had always been a perfect gentleman toward me so what did it matter? And finally there were the two thoughts that kept creeping into my mind. Did George have a thing for heels, or was it me he was thinking about, and why oh why did I keep thinking about that fat cock he was playing with? By the time I reached work the next morning I had made up my mind to keep my mouth shut, keep quiet about things and just live and let live.

***

Over the next few weeks I found several opportunities to watch George jack off using my heels. I got to the point where I would finger myself while watching and I always made it a point to wear the shoes he jacked off into at work the next day. My husband still thought that the situation was comical and he started telling me that I should, "Go on in and help the poor guy out." I got upset with him for even thinking that I could do such a thing and that just made him laugh more. And then one night, on an impulse that came from I know not where, I walked in on George. He was stunned. He froze in mid-stroke and stared at me. I put a finger to my lips to indicate that I didn't want him to say a word and I told him to just be quiet and enjoy. I walked over to his desk and sat on the edge. I kicked off my tennis shoes and put my feet around his cock, rubbed it a few times and then told him to take hold of my feet and jack himself off with them. I leaned back on the desk and fingered myself to an orgasm as I watched him work on himself with my feet. I could tell from the increase in pressure he put on my feet and the increase in the speed of his strokes and I started to talk to him.

"Cum for me baby, cum on my feet, cum for me" and he obliged by shooting a thick stream of cum all over my feet. I got off the desk and stepped into my pumps and then I walked around the office in them for a minute or so and then I took them off and set them in the middle of his desk. I peeled off my nylons and set them on the desk next to the shoes.

"I'll see you in the morning George" and I left the office.

***

I could not believe what I had done. I was a virgin when I married my husband and the only cock I had ever or touched was his, and here, out of a clear blue sky, I'd let another man use my feet to masturbate with. I didn't just let him; I instigated the whole thing.

The second surprise of the night came when I confessed what I had done to my husband. He was so turned on by my description of what I had done that he pulled me down and fucked me right on the living room floor. When we went to bed that night he had me tell him the story again and when I did he fucked me for an hour.

In the morning he asked me if I was going to do it again and when I told him that I would probably go to work and find out that I'd been fired he laughed.

"Oh no you won't! He will probably be waiting for you in his office tonight and what might get you fired is not showing up."

"But what about us? I cheated on you last night. Don't you care that your wife let another man use her sexually?"

"You didn't fuck him so as far as I'm concerned you didn't cheat, and as far as "us" is concerned I think the way I reacted last night should have shown you that we are all right."

Still, the next morning I went to work in a very nervous condition. George, however, did not behave any differently toward me than he usually did. When I came back from lunch I found a package on my desk. Inside was a pair of red high heels in my size, six pair of nylons and an unsigned card that said, "Thank you for being so understanding."

***

I had every intention of being the first person out of the office that night and to never spy on George again, but when five o'clock rolled around I found myself stalling until everyone else was gone. I put on my new red high heels and walked into George's office. He was talking to his wife on the phone and I walked up to him and pushed his chair back from the desk. I bent over, undid his belt, unzipped his fly and then pulled his trousers and his briefs off of him. Sitting on his desk I reached out with my high heel clad feet and started rubbing his cock. He made excuses to his wife, hung up the phone and then both hands took hold of my feet and he masturbated himself to orgasm while I leaned back on the desk and used my fingers to get myself off. When he had unloaded himself all over my feet I stood up, stepped out of my shoes, peeled off my nylons and put them on the desk and then I headed for the front door. During the entire episode not one word had been said by either of us.

That night after I told my husband what I had done he went crazy and fucked me four times. That was the most he had ever been able to do and the poor dear was totally exhausted when he fell asleep.

That set the pattern for the next three weeks. Two or three times a week after everyone else went home I went into George's office for a mutual masturbation session. Sometimes he would use my nylon clad feet, sometimes he would leave my heels on and use them and sometimes I would take off my nylons and he would wrap them around his cock and jack off. George never spoke during these sessions and I limited my conversation to what was required to let him know what I wanted (which basically amounted to, "Cum for me baby, cum for me, etc., etc., etc…"). Once a week or so I would get a package with anywhere from six to twelve pair of nylons and occasionally a new pair of pumps and every night I would go home and tell my husband what I had done that day and then he would spend the night trying to fuck me to death.

***

Last Wednesday I entered George's office and found him on the phone with his wife. He motioned for me to leave, but for some reason a streak of wickedness decided to show itself. I unzipped him and took out his cock – my feet were all that had touched his cock till then – and then I looked up into his eyes, smiled and started to jack him off. I could feel his cock throb as I worked it and I kept my eyes on his as he tried to hold a conversation with his wife. He dropped a hand down to take hold of his cock, but I pushed it away and started talking to him.

"Going to cum for me baby? Going to give me your cum? Come on George, give it to me. Shake your head George, let me know when you're going to cum. Think of my sexy feet George, think of my sexy toes, think of my high heel rubbing your cock. Come on George, cum for me."

Pretty soon George was shaking his head and I picked up the speed of my stroke as I reached down and took off my right high heel. I missed the first spurt, but I caught the rest in my shoe and set it on the desk. I continued to pump George until he went limp. I took off my nylons and used them to wipe him off and then I put my shoe back on and walked around the office. His eyes followed me as he kept on talking to his wife. I went back to the desk and sat down on the edge. I kicked off my pumps and started to masturbate myself. I did not hear George hang up the phone. The first I was aware that he was not still talking to his wife was when I felt a tingle in my foot and I looked to see George licking the cum from between my toes. When his tongue slid between my toes I had a tremendous orgasm and when I recovered I left my nylons and pumps on George's desk, went and put on my tennis shoes and ran home.

My husband was a maniac that night. He fucked me so hard and for so long that I wondered if I would be able to walk to work the next day. In the morning he hit me with the bombshell. He wanted to come down to my office after closing and watch. I was leery at first, but I finally agreed that I would let him in on Friday.

The next two sessions with George were a repeat. I masturbated George into one of my pumps, walked around in them, and then masturbated myself while George licked the cum off my feet.

***

Friday after everyone else was gone I unlocked the front door and let my husband in. I warned him to be very quiet and then I went into George's office. The session started out with George using my feet to masturbate with. After a minute or so I got off the desk, knelt in front of him and started jacking him off with my hands. I had a high heel ready to catch the cum when George ejaculated, but at the last minute, just as the first spurt of sperm was leaving the head of his cock, and knowing that my husband was watching, I bent and took George's cock into my mouth and I sucked on it and licked it until it went limp. Without looking up at George's face I got up and left the office and went home where my husband kept me on my back damned near the entire weekend.

I suspect that I might have altered the relationship I had with George, but I won't know until I go to work on Monday. My husband wants me to bring George home for dinner some night. If I still have a job come next week, who knows? It just might be fun.

The End

Belinda Screws Up

I saw her in the rearview mirror, standing there looking as if she were just about to be hit by a runaway freight train. It was a miserable way to end a marriage of over twenty years, but I had given her a chance and it wasn't my fault that she made the wrong choice.

***

Belinda and I had met at my cousin's wedding reception. She was a friend of the bride's and had come to the wedding with a date. I took one look at her and knew – just knew – that she was meant to be my life partner. I ignored the fact that she was there with a date and I moved in on her. I asked her to dance when her date went off to use the bathroom and as we moved around on the dance floor I told her that I hoped her date wasn't too attached to her because I intended to make her mine. She laughed and said:

"Really?"

"Yes really?"

"Well in that case I hope you have a good memory" and she told me her phone number.

While I was committing the number to memory she said, "Oops, here comes Jeff and I am his date."

I walked her back to the table she was sharing with some friends and she introduced me to them and then she gave me a wicked smile and said to those at the table:

"Remember the name. He says he is going to make me his. If he manages you just might see him around."

That got a few laughs from the people at the table and a murderous stare from Jeff. I raised her hand to my lips, kissed it and said, "I'll call you."

I called, we started dating and a year later we were married. Over the course of the next twenty years we had a very good life together. She bore me three children, two boys and a girl, and she did a marvelous job of raising them and spoiling me.

***

Our youngest had just departed for basic training and Belinda was at loose ends so she went looking for a job. She found a job as a secretary for a local auto parts company and she had been on the job two weeks when one morning she told me that she was going to be late that night. I asked her why and she told me that she was going to stop after work for drinks with some of the girls she worked with to get to know them better. I didn't even think twice about it, I just said:

"Have a good time sweetie."

"Thank you honey, I'll try not to be too late."

I'm normally in bed by nine-thirty because I get up at five so I told her not to wake me when she got home. The next day I asked her how her night had gone and she told me that she'd had a good time.

"There are a lot of nice people working there. Honey, would it bother you if I joined their little group? They stop every Thursday night after work and I'd really like to get to know them better."

Why would I mind? I had my bowling league on Thursday and I wouldn't be home until nine anyway so I told Belinda to go ahead and enjoy. A couple of months went by and sometimes Belinda would be home when I got home from bowling and sometimes she wouldn't get in until after I had gone to bed. I didn't think anything of it. Why should I?

We had been married for over twenty years and Belinda had never given me any reason to wonder or worry about what she was doing.

The dark clouds started appearing on the horizon about five months after she had started her job. I didn't recognize them as such at the time, but looking back I can almost pin point the time that things began to change. Belinda was always talking about the people she worked with; about how this guy was this and this woman was that and so and so did such and such. The one she talked the most about was Carla.

Carla was three times divorced and was currently single and she swore she would never tie herself down with a man again. She dated a lot, had no steady boyfriend and my take on her, from what Belinda told me, was that she was a round-heeled tramp. Apparently she and Belinda had become good friends and Carla would share her exploits with Belinda who would then pass them on to me over the dinner table.

"You'll never guess what crazy Carla did Monday night. She and James, I told you about James didn't I? Anyway, she and James had stopped at a bar after work and after about an hour James took her to his place. She had never been there before and she didn't know that he had a roommate. She and James were having sex when the roommate walked in on them. It was an awkward moment, but Carla diffused it by saying that she had enough for both of them. Can you believe it? Both of them? I can't even imagine something like that."

A week later on a Friday night it was, "You know what Carla did last night? A guy she'd never met before asked her to dance and an hour later she left the bar with him. Thirty minutes later she was back and Barb said, "What's the matter, find out he had a wife and dump him?" Carla said, "No, I did him on his back seat and then he took off." Isn't that just outrageous?"

I got one or two of those stories every week, but the light bulb never went off over my head. I could never understand what Belinda saw in Carla and how the two of them could get so close that Carla would share her sex life with Belinda. I supposed that it must have been an opposites attract kind of thing. After a couple of months of being regaled with Carla stories I made the comment that she sounded like a real whore.

"That's probably the reason she has been divorced three times; got her ass caught cheating."

Belinda didn't say anything to that, but the Carla stories stopped.

***

A little more time went by and one day I read in the paper that the auto parts company that Belinda worked for was having some financial problems and that bankruptcy was possible. I mentioned it to Belinda and asked if it was going to affect her.

"It could if they actually have to go Chapter 11, but we are all hopeful that it won't happen."

The next day she told me that it was going to affect her after all. "They are reorganizing and it is going to mean that I'm going to have to work late some nights"

"What does that mean, some nights?"

"I guess it means that some nights I'm going to be asked to stay late."

"Oh well, I guess it goes with the job. I just hope the extra effort pays off for you."

"I hope so too. I like the job and I like the people I work with and I don't want to have to start over again someplace else."

Two days later she called me on my cell and told me that she would be working late that night. I asked her how late and she said she didn't have any idea, but they had told everybody they were going to order take out around seven.

"All right sweetie. If you aren't home by the time I go to bed I'll see you in the morning."

After that, one or two nights a week Belinda had to work late. There was no more in the papers about the parts company so I guessed that whatever they were doing as far as reorganizing was working. A couple of more months went by and then it was the end of bowling until the summer leagues started. I went home after work and around seven I got tired of watching TV so I decided to go down to the lounge, have a drink or two with my wife and meet a few of her co-workers.

I walked into the lounge and looked around the room for Belinda and finally spotted her out on the dance floor with some guy. They were dancing pretty close and I saw the man's hand slide down her back and come to rest on her ass. When she didn't push the hand away or step back from the man I suddenly decided not to have a drink with her after all. Instead, I looked for a nice dark corner to sit in.

For the next two hours I sat there, sipped beer and watched as Belinda danced with the same man. When I first came in he walked her back to a table where she was apparently sitting with a half dozen other girls, but after a half-hour or so and three or four dances she went to the booth with him where he had been sitting.

For the next hour and a half she stayed with him. Every time they danced Belinda was molded to his body and his hands were all over hers. I was getting more and more steamed by the minute and the only thing that kept me from going over and raining on their parade was that I wanted to know more about what was going on. When they finished a dance and went back to the booth and she slid in next to him instead of sitting across from him and then kissed him I got up and went outside. I got in my car and moved it to where I could see Belinda's car and then I sat and waited to see what would happen next.

I had no idea how long I was going to have to wait because I had no idea of when Belinda usually came home. If she wasn't there before I fell asleep I usually slept too soundly for her to wake me up when she came in. It could have been ten or it could have been three in the morning. It was ten-thirty when Belinda came out of the bar with the people she had originally been sitting with before joining the man in his booth. The group scattered to their cars and drove off.

Belinda got in her car and sat there for about five minutes before the man came out of the bar and got in the car with her. They talked for about five minutes and then they slid towards each other and started necking. From where I was sitting I could see Belinda's sweater when it was pushed up on her shoulders and that told me that the man's hands were on her tits, but I couldn't actually see what his hands, or hers, were doing. What I thought I saw was arm motion that indicated that the man was getting a hand job from Belinda.

Whatever they were doing they did it and necked for about the next fifteen minutes and then they separated, talked for several more minutes and then the man got out of her car, got into his and drove off. As soon as he was gone Belinda got out of her car and went back into the bar and I assumed that it was so she could straighten herself up before coming home just in case I might still be up. As soon as the door closed behind her I started up and drove home. I was in bed pretending to be asleep when Belinda got home twenty minutes later.

***

I didn't say anything to Belinda about what I'd seen and for the next week I did my best to act as if everything was normal. The next Thursday I was back in the dark corner wearing as much of a disguise as I could come up with. I had been wearing contacts for about fifteen years so I bought a pair of reading glasses with heavy horn-rimmed frames and punched the lens out. I have never worn a hat so I got a baseball cap and pulled the bill down low to block part of my face. Not much, but since Belinda was used to seeing me without glasses and a hat and I was sitting in a dark corner I thought I could get by.

She came in about a quarter to six with the same group of women she had been sitting with the previous Thursday and they put three tables together right next to the dance floor. For the next hour until the band started up at seven the group sat, talked and had drinks. Belinda sat next to and talked mostly with a dark haired woman and I thought she might be Carla.

The band started to play and guys started going over to the table and asking the girls to dance. Belinda danced with two or three different guys, but didn't seem to show an interest in any of them. About eight a guy asked the woman I thought might be Carla to dance and when the music stopped she went back to the booth where he had been sitting with two buddies and sat down with him. She danced with all three of the men and all three of them danced real close with her and felt her up pretty good and then she necked with all three when she went back to their booth. During that period Belinda danced with three different guys, but didn't seem interested in them.

Around nine Carla went over to the table and talked for a minute with Belinda and then Belinda got up and followed Carla back to the booth and sat down with her and the three men. Over the next forty-five minutes Belinda danced with all three of the men and they treated her much as they had Carla and she necked in the booth with them as Carla had.

At five to ten Carla and two of the men got up and left and Belinda was left sitting in the booth across from the remaining man and he got up and moved to sit beside her. They necked for a bit, danced a couple of dances and then went back to the booth and necked some more. When Belinda got up to go to the ladies room I got up and left the bar. I moved my car to where I could watch Belinda's car and settled down to wait.

Twenty minutes went by and then Belinda and the man came out and stopped just outside the door and talked for a minute and then they headed away from me to the other end of the lot and got into his car. I couldn't see much from where I was sitting, but I could see them sitting and talking and then they slid together and started necking. It went on for about twenty minutes and then they broke apart, got out of his car and walked to Belinda's. They talked for another minute and then he took her in his arms and kissed her. They stayed locked together for almost a minute and then they broke apart and Belinda got in her car and he went back to his. He started and drove off and as soon as he was out of sight Belinda got out of her car and went back into the bar to freshen up and that time I stayed and waited. She came out ten minutes later, got in her car and headed for home.

I let her go and then I went back into the lounge for a drink. I sat at the bar and struck up a conversation with the bartender.

"I may have to start coming in here more often."

"Why is that?"

"I've been in here twice now and both times I've seen a lot of action going on with the girls at that table over there."

"It sure looks like it, don't it?"

"I'm always looking for a fun time. Do they come in here often?"

"Every Thursday night."

"Only on Thursday?"

"Two of them, Carla and Belinda are in here on other nights, but the rest of them only come in on Thursday."

I left him a tip and told him I was going to become a Thursday regular from then on. Driving home the thought occurred to me that Belinda wasn't working the nights she said she was. Those nights had to be the 'other nights' that the bartender told me Belinda came in.

Belinda was still up when I got home. "Where have you been? When I got home and you weren't here I got worried."

"Tonight was the last night of bowling and the guys stuck around to have a few beers and discuss what we want to do as far as a summer league is concerned."

"When do summer leagues start?"

"Next week."

"What did you decide?"

"Haven't yet. Dave and Sam want to move to Wednesday and Chuck and Bill want to stay with Thursday."

"Sounds like you get to be the tie breaker. What do you want to do?"

"I don't really care, but I'm leaning toward Wednesday."

"I think you should stay with Thursday."

"Why?"

"Because that is the night I stop with the girls. It just makes sense for our nights out to be the same."

Right, I thought, that way I won't be sitting at home wondering what you might be doing because I'd be occupied.

"I hadn't looked at it that way. I suppose that you are right."

"Anyway, I'm glad you are home. I'm horny as hell. That give you any ideas?"

Actually it did. I was curious to see if my dick would get hard considering the thoughts that I was having about Belinda. It was slow to show, but a Belinda blow job got me up and running and I guess I performed well enough to suit her.

***

Monday she called me on my cell and told me she had to work late. I left work early and was parked just down the street from where she worked when she came out of the building with Carla. They both got into Belinda's car and I wasn't at all surprised when Belinda headed for the lounge. I followed them and parked in the back where I could watch Belinda's car and then I settled in to wait.

Three hours later Carla and Belinda came out with the same three men from Thursday night. Carla got in back with the two who had left with her and the one Belinda had necked with got in front with her. Belinda started the car and I got ready to follow, but Belinda didn't leave the lot; she just drove to the back of the lot and pulled in behind the dumpster. I couldn't see anything from where I was, but it was dark out and even darker behind the dumpster so I got out of the car and tried to work my way closer to Belinda's car without being seen.

I couldn't do it. The half moon in the clear night gave just enough light that I would be seen if I went around either end of the dumpster. I noticed that the dumpster lids, which were propped open, had large cutouts around the hinge points and I wondered if I could see anything if I climbed inside the dumpster and looked through one of the cutouts. The moon was on the other side of Belinda's car so I wouldn't be back lit if anyone in the car happened to glance toward the cutout. I thought that I would give it a try before going to Plan B which was to walk up to the car, rap on the window and ask Belinda just what the fuck she was doing.

Hoping that I wouldn't step into anything stinky I quietly climbed into the dumpster and moved to the center cutout. I had a perfect view down into the car and the moonlight let me get a good look.

Carla was on the backseat on her knees, skirt up around her waist, and her head was bobbing up and down on the cock sticking up out of one guy's fly. The second guy was behind her and he had his pants down around his ankles and his cock buried in her from behind. From my angle I couldn't tell if he was in her cunt or her ass.

In the front seat Belinda's blouse was open and her bra was undone and the man with her had his right tit in his mouth. His cock was sticking out of his fly and Belinda had her had on it and she was stroking him as she looked over the back of the seat at what was going on in back. The man she was jacking off said something and she turned to look at him and said something. He said something and I saw Belinda shake her head no. The man said something else and put a hand on Belinda's head and tried to push it down on his cock. She let go of his dick and slapped his hand away from her. The windows of the car were closed so I couldn't hear what was going on, but I did hear the:

"God damn it, I said no!" so she really must have screamed it at him.

He pulled back from her and Belinda let her bra slip off and fall to the floor and she buttoned up her blouse.

In the back the man fucking Carla finished and he pulled out of her and then there was a major reshuffle in the car as she took her mouth off the man she was sucking and the men all changed position. The man up front moved to the back and sat down so Carla could suck him while the man she had been sucking got behind her to fuck her. The man with the limp dick moved up front and started talking to Belinda as she looked into the back and watched as Carla serviced the two men.

After a couple of minutes of talking the man in front with Belinda slid a little closer to her, put an arm around her and kissed her. They necked for a bit and I saw him unbutton her blouse and start playing with her tits. His limp dick was still sticking out of his fly and he took Belinda's hand and put it on his cock and she started fondling it.

For several minutes Belinda necked with the man while he played with her tits and his dick grew hard in her hand.

The man fucking Carla came and pulled out of her and then moved up front and Belinda ended up sitting in the middle between two men. Carla rolled over on her back and spread her legs for the man she had been sucking and he shoved his cock into her. I noticed for the first time that Carla was wearing spiked heels and her legs were pointing straight up as the man fucked her and I wondered if her heels would poke a hole in the headliner.

When I turned my attention back to the front seat I saw that the two men were working on Belinda. They had her legs pulled apart and her skirt pushed up to her waist and the one on the left was kissing her and finger fucking her while the one on the right was sucking on one tit and rolling the nipple of the other between his fingers. Belinda had a cock in each hand and she was stroking them both.

The man kissing her broke the kiss and Belinda laid her head against the back of the seat, eyes closed, as the two men worked on her. The man on the right kissed her, then the man on the left and then back to the one on the right. Just as both men took turns kissing her they took turns finger fucking her and sucking on her tits.

She was kissing the man on her left when suddenly she jerked her face away from him and looked to the right. I saw that the man on her right had cum on her leg. She said something and the man on the right said something and she brought her hand up and looked at it. Cum was dripping off her fingers and she looked at the hand for a couple of seconds and then she licked her hand clean.

The man on the right said something and then laughed and then the man on the left said something and Belinda turned her attention to him. Her left hand let go of his cock and she took it in her right hand and started beating him off while the two of them swapped tongues. In less than a minute he shot his wad, Belinda licked her hand clean and then began wiping up the mess with her skirt.

By the time Belinda had gotten the man on her left off Carla and the man fucking her had finished and they were rearranging their clothes. The man on Belinda's right had put his cock away and zipped up and so I guessed they were getting ready to go. I quietly climbed out of the dumpster and headed back to my car and then waited to see what would happen next.

Several minutes later Belinda pulled out from behind the dumpster and parked by the door of the bar. Everyone got out and headed into the bar, but before Belinda followed them she opened the truck of the car and got out a bag and took it into the bar with her. Twenty minutes later Belinda and Carla came out, got in the car and drove off and I started up my car and drove home.

As I drove home I thought about what I had just witnessed. Belinda had abandoned herself to the mouths and hands of three men and had had three different cocks in her hand, two of which she had jacked off to completion. She had vehemently said no to a blow job and in the three times I had managed to watch her she had not been fucked. I suppose what she was doing was cheating, but I had to ask myself if it was 'bad' cheating. Was she just having some vicarious fun and thinking as long as she didn't fuck them and suck them it was okay?

I don't know what she was thinking, but I do know what I thought about it. She was lying to me and had been for several months. She was not working late and her girl's night out was a lot more than just that. Even if she hadn't fucked or sucked the men she had gone out to the parking lot with, how many hand jobs had she given? How many times had she licked some guy off her fingers and then come home to me and kissed me? And what was I going to do about it?

***

If I was right Belinda would be coming home hotter than a forest fire and wanting to fuck. I debated being in bed and pretending to be asleep, but in the end I decided to be mean. I was in the kitchen when Belinda got home and when she walked in she said:

"Oh goody, you're up" and she went to kiss me and I turned my face away from her. She pulled back and said, "Why did you do that?"

"You need to do something about your breath."

She looked at me for a second and then said, "I guess I'd better hurry up and do it then since I'm horny as hell and intend to take advantage of the fact that you are up."

"Not tonight sweetie. I've had a miserable headache almost all day. That's why I'm still up; it hurts my head to lie down."

She was clearly upset that she wasn't going to get her itch scratched, but what could she do but accept it like I had to when she used the headache excuse on me.

"Well I'm going to bed then, I hope you feel better in the morning" and she headed for the bedroom.

I went into the living room, picked up a magazine and read it until I thought Belinda had been in bed long enough to fall asleep and then I went to the bedroom and checked. She was softly snoring away so I got her car keys from her purse and went out to her car. I opened the trunk and saw two bags. I checked one and saw that it held the cum covered nylons she had been wearing and the skirt she had used to wipe things up with.

The other bag had a couple of changes of underwear, nylons, two skirts and a blouse. Down at the bottom of the bag were six still wrapped condoms. If she hadn't already done it, Belinda was clearly getting ready to fuck someone. I put everything back where I found it, closed the trunk and then went back inside the house and went to bed.

***

In the morning I was up and out of the house before Belinda woke up. I spent most of my day at work thinking about what to do. I decided to go straight at it. That night when I got home Belinda asked me how my head was and I said I was fine.

"Did you take aspirin or something? You seemed to be sleeping soundly when I got up to go to the bathroom."

"I didn't have a headache last night, I just didn't want to fuck you."

That got her attention because I'd never used that word with her before. For over twenty years we had made love, we had never fucked. She gave me a strange look and then asked:

"Why didn't you want to make love to me?"

"I didn't want sloppy seconds."

Her face got red and she angrily snapped, "How dare you accuse me of something like that?"

"Where were you last night?"

"I was working late. You know that because I called you at work and told you."

"Yes, and you were lying through your teeth," I said as I got ready to tell one of my own. "I worked late last night and I thought it might be a nice idea to stop and get some take out, drop by your place, have a quick bite to eat with you before going home. Imagine my surprise to find the place locked up tight, no lights on and the parking lot empty. So tell me Belinda, who were you with and what were you doing?"

She was silent for several seconds and then she said, "I went out and had a few drinks with Carla."

"Carla and who else?"

"Nobody else, just me and Carla."

"And all those other nights you said you were working late?"

"Spending time with Carla."

"Just Carla?

"Yes."

"And what did you and 'just Carla' do?"

"We just went out for drinks and talked."

"And for that you had to lie to me?"

"You made your feeling about her clear when you called her a round heeled whore. I thought it would be best if I never brought her name up any more. She's my friend, I like her, I like talking to her and I like spending time with her. You don't like what you were hearing about her so I kept it from you."

"And I'm supposed to accept that? You tell me how big a slut she is and then you go and run with her and I'm supposed to just accept it when you tell me that all you do is drink and talk?"

"It's true."

"I don't believe you, but I have too much invested in this marriage to push it. I am going to say that I don't want associating with her anymore."

"I'm forty-three years old John; I'm way past having other people decide who I can be friends with and who I can't."

"That gets to be your choice then. Your marriage or your friend. Here is how I see it. I've been the only man in your life and you listen to Carla tell you about all the fun she is having with all the guys and it makes you curious about other men. That will eventually lead you to try another man or two, if you haven't already, and I won't live with that. You keep running with Carla and you will kill your marriage. You get to make the choice."

"Damn it John, that's not fair. I told you I haven't done anything and I don't intend to."

"I've said my piece Belinda. It is all on you now" and I got up from the table and went out into the garage to change the oil and spark plug on the lawn mower.

***

I was giving her a free ride on what she had already done. I was pissed at her, but you don't just throw away a marriage that had been good for twenty-three years. I had convinced myself that she hadn't yet let another man fuck her even though the condoms in her trunk told me she was considering it. I could get over the necking and the hand jobs, but I knew if she kept hanging with Carla it was only a matter of time until those condoms started to get used. I'd made my speech and my position on the matter should be crystal clear to Belinda so all I could do was wait and see.

It was three the next afternoon when Belinda called me at work. "I just wanted to let you know I'll be late getting home tonight."

"Oh? Working late again?" I said sarcastically."

"No John, Carla and I are going to stop for drinks."

"Okay Belinda, just remember, it was your choice" and I hung up on her.

I walked down to the boss's office and told him I need to leave early to take care of a personal problem. I stopped by a storage place and bought some boxes and by nine that night I had everything that I wanted out of the house and was checked into a motel. I turned off my cell phone and went to bed.

I hadn't been at work five minutes the next morning when Belinda called me on the phone.

"What did you do John?"

"I moved out."

"Why in God's name did you do that?"

"I told you that the choice was yours Belinda. I made it as plain as I could that the choice was your marriage or Carla and at three in the afternoon yesterday you called me and told me that your choice was Carla. Now if you'll excuse me I have to get to work."

"You are being absolutely unreasonable John."

"I don't think so Belinda. Good-bye" and I hung up on her. The phone rang almost immediately and I saw from caller ID that it was Belinda so I didn't answer it. She called a dozen more times during the day and I didn't take one of them.

She was waiting for me in the parking lot when I got off work.

"We need to talk John."

"No we don't. I said my piece the other night."

"John, I don't know where your head is, but you are off your rocker if you think that my associating with Carla is going to make me cheat on you."

"Define cheating for me Belinda. What is and what isn't cheating?"

"Having affairs with other men."

"Is that all? Aren't there other forms of cheating also?"

"What are you getting at John?"

"Let me give you a few examples Belinda and then you tell me if they are cheating or not cheating. A married woman leaves a bar with a man who is not her husband, gets in a car with him and necks with him for half an hour. Is that cheating? How about while they are necking he plays with her tits and she gives him a hand job; is that cheating?"

She just stared at me and I could swear that I read "what does he know" in her eyes. "Well, what is your answer?"

"She doesn't make love to the man?"

"No."

"Then she isn't really cheating."

"See Belinda, that is where we differ. I think it is cheating."

"What has that got to do with us and the situation that we are in?"

"It is what you did Belinda. It is what you did the three times that I know of and God only knows how many other times."

She was indignant, "How in the hell can you accuse me of something like that?"

"Easy Belinda, I watched. Bowling has been over for three weeks now. Two weeks ago since I didn't have to bowl I thought I'd stop in at the lounge, have a couple of drinks with you and meet some of your co-workers. When I walked in you were out on the dance floor with some guy and he was feeling you up and you were doing nothing to stop him. I moved to a dark corner and I sat and watched you and I was in the parking lot watching you when he got in your car with you and you did what you did."

I saw her face go pale as what I was telling her registered on her. "The next Thursday I was back in that same dark corner when you and your group walked in and I watched you in the booth with Carla and the three guys and I was outside in my car when you went and got in the man's car and I saw what you did."

I stared at her for a few seconds and then said, "You cheated on me Belinda. You can say that what you did wasn't cheating all you want, but to me it was. Why do you have rubbers in the trunk of your car?"

"What?"

"Simple question Belinda, why do you have rubbers in the trunk of your car?"

"You are out of your mind John."

I snatched her purse away from her and took out her car keys. I walked over to the trunk of her car and put the key in the lock. "Are you sure I'm out of my mind Belinda? When I open this trunk what am I going to find?"

She just stared at me without saying a word so I popped open the trunk. There were the same two bags. I picked up the smaller of the two and dumped it out. There was a skirt, a thong and a pair of nylons and they all had traces of dried cum on them.

"What's this Belinda?" and I held up the stained pair of nylons.

She just stared at me wordlessly and I dropped the nylons and picked up the other bag. "This bag had six condoms in it the other night. How many are there in there now Belinda? Are there still six in there now, or did some get used last night while you were out having, what was it you said, having drinks with Carla?"

I dropped the bag back in the trunk as I said, "I don't really want to know how many rubbers are in the bag Belinda. If it is any less than six I don't know what I might do. You still haven't answered my question Belinda, why do you have condoms in the trunk? And while I am on the subject, why are there cum stained nylons, a cum stained skirt and a cum stained thong in your trunk?"

I closed the trunk and walked over to her and handed her the keys and then I walked around her and opened the door to my car. Behind me I heard her say:

"It isn't what you think John, I can explain."

I turned to face her and said, "Okay, I'm listening."

"That stuff is Carla's. She doesn't have a car so when we go out I drive and she keeps that stuff in the trunk."

"The cum stained clothes?"

"You've heard me talk about her John, about how wild she is. A lot of the times we go out she will go out in the parking lot with some guy and she always has spare clothes in case things get messy."

"And you don't understand why I didn't want you around her?"

"I'm a grown woman John and I can take care of myself. Just because Carla is wild doesn't mean I will be."

"So you maintain that the clothes and rubbers are Carla's?"

"Yes."

"Carla doesn't use rubbers Belinda. Not one rubber was used when she fucked those three men on your back seat while you were parked behind the dumpster the other night."

I saw the shock register on her face.

"That's right Belinda, I saw it all. What Carla did on the back seat and what you did on the front seat. I watched you use your skirt to clean up the mess and I saw you go back into the bar and change out of the dirty skirt into a clean one. Those cum stained clothes are yours, not Carla's. While I'm on the subject, the other night behind the dumpster you were wearing white cotton undies so that means the cum stained thong is from last night. What do you have to say now Belinda? I still want you to tell me why you have condoms."

She didn't say a word, just stood there and looked at me like a deer caught in the headlights of a car.

"I knew all of this when we talked night before last. You want to know why I turned my head when you tried to kiss me? I had just finished watching you lick the cum of two men off your fingers. No way was I going to let your mouth touch mine after that."

I thought I saw her getting ready to tear up on me. She knew that I hated to see her cry and she was getting ready to try and use that fact to get to me, but it wasn't going to work this time.

"Even knowing that Belinda, even knowing everything that I'd found out and seen on the three nights I watched you I sucked it up and put it behind me to try and save our marriage. All I asked was that you put an end to what you were doing with Carla. I gave you a "Get out of jail free" card Belinda and last night you tore it up and threw it away. At three o'clock yesterday afternoon you called me and told me that you were choosing your nights fucking around in parking lots over our marriage. Marriage over, I moved out. It is as simple as that."

I got in my car, started it up and drove away while she stood there and watched me go.

The End

Alana Asserts Herself

I sat in my office staring out the window with thoughts of murder on my mind. Murder would be the quickest way to go and it would definitely be the most satisfying, but I also know that there is no such thing as the Perfect Crime - not for an ordinary guy like me anyway - and I have no desire to go to jail. Who would I like to do in? My loving wife of course, and all because we both love sex.

Alana and I married after a whirlwind courtship. We met at a cocktail party in LA on a Thursday night, spent all of Friday and half a day Saturday in bed and then drove to Vegas and were married on Saturday night. I know, I can hear it now, "You met and got married in the space of twenty-four hours and you got marriage problems? Well duh!"

Actually that would be a wrong assumption on the reader's part. Alana and I were made for each other and the marriage lasted more than ten years trouble free. It has been in only the last three months that things have gone to hell and, admittedly, it is as much my fault as Alana's that things have gone bad. As I mentioned before, both Alana and I love sex and are always trying on new things to add spice to an already spicy marriage. The trouble started when we decided to add role playing to our repertoire. It began with simple stuff like Alana going into a bar and acting like a prostitute looking for a John and letting me pick her up in front of all the people there. I'd fix her car and she would pretend I was the mechanic at the garage and she would offer to fuck me in place of paying her bill. We tried the burglar surprising the lady of the house in bed, the service man coming to fix the (fill in the blank) and the lady of the house fucking him because she didn't have the check book and had no cash. Then we progressed to light bondage and Alana would have me tie her to the bed, use a feather and dildos on her and then fuck her.

After a while we discussed the possibility of taking on a third person, male or female, it didn't matter, as long as it added spice to the marriage. We were both secure enough that we felt we could handle so we tried it with another woman and it was great. Then we tried it with another guy and it was just as great. We limited our use of extra partners to once a month, more with the idea of keeping things new and exciting than anything else and it worked out well for us. There were two women and three guys that we used on a rotating basis and for two years things went along fine.

As I said, the trouble began about three months ago and I have only myself to blame for it. I had been gone on an extended business trip and Alana had been without sex for almost two weeks. I know that that doesn't sound like a long time, but for a woman used to getting laid five and six times a week it can seem like forever. I was due to be gone another four days, maybe five, and during my nightly call to Alana she told me she was climbing walls and she asked me if she could please call one of our three studs in waiting. I saw no harm in that so I told her to go ahead. When I called her the next night she thanked me for letting her 'get settled down' and then she said, "The boys damn near wore me out."

"The boys?" I asked.

It seems that Dave and Fred were not answering their phones and when she called Todd he said he couldn't come over because he had an out of town guest - his old college roommate was staying with him. Alana was so desperate that she told Todd to bring his buddy along with him and the two of them had worked her over most of the night.

"I knew you wouldn't mind," she said, "and now I should be able to hang on until you get home."

Didn't think I'd mind? Of course I minded. I was letting other guys fuck my wife, but I'd always had some say in the matter. I'd always checked them out before granting approval and I didn't know anything about this friend of Todd's. I was pissed, but I kept a rein on my emotions and told Alana that I would be home in two days and that, unlike her, I had gone without and she was going to have to take up the slack when I got home.

We fucked up a storm the first five days I was back and then we fell back into our normal routine. At the end of the month, when it was our usual time to bring in a third person, she told me that she wanted to do Todd and his buddy, "I've never had three men at once and I think it would be fun."

I wasn't all that keen on the idea, but it was Alana's body and I didn't feel that I could tell her that she couldn't have what she wanted, at least not since we had opened the door to extra partners. Given that I'd not been given the chance to check out Tim before allowing him to join our little circle I was predisposed to dislike him before he even walked in the door. When he and Todd arrived I took an instant dislike to him and it didn't help that he had a permanent smirk on his face or that his attitude toward me was condescending. He acted as if he was there to do me a favor. Alana positively gushed over him and I soon found out why - he had a cock that would have done a stud horse proud. I suddenly understood why Alana had been so insistent on having him come back with Todd. Don't kid yourself by thinking that size doesn't count. The only people who say that are the women who can't get one or the guys that don't have a big one. For Alana's sake I kept my thoughts about Tim to myself and let the evening proceed. I do admit to a certain amount of fascination as I watched Alana taking every single inch of that monster cock and then beg to be fucked harder. When the two guys left in the morning Alana couldn't even walk; I had to carry her to the bathroom. The next day I told Alana that I didn't like the "arrogant bastard" and that I didn't want him coming back. Alana didn't say anything and I thought that was the end of the matter.

The next three weeks were normal, nothing but straight sex and plenty of it, and then one night I came home from work to find Alana wearing her vinyl corset and black high heeled boots. It was her way of telling me that tonight was going to be a 'light bondage night' and that it was my turn to submit. She ordered me to disrobe and then had me sit on one of our straight back dining room chairs and then she tied my arms and legs to the chair. Next she tied a blindfold over my eyes and said, "Tonight slave, you will learn to suck a cock. I'm going to parade all of my lovers past you and after you have sucked all their cocks you will identify them. If you correctly name them all I will allow you to fuck me tonight. If you fail, you can go to bed by yourself and play with your miserable excuse for a cock."

I heard her leave the room and when she came back I felt something push at my lips, "Open your mouth slave and treat my lover's manhood with the respect that it deserves."

I stuck my tongue out and touched the thing she was holding and she said, "Suck it slave!" I opened my mouth and something rubbery was pushed in. Since I had never sucked a cock in my life and had no way of knowing how all I could do was treat it the way I liked mine to be treated. After a minute or so Alana asked, "Who is it slave?"

Alana has a collection of dildos and she has named each one and I guessed that my task was going to be to identify each one correctly. The one I'd just had in my mouth was small, almost cigar sized, and so I said, "That was Mr. Rectum."

Alana snorted and said, "Lucky guess."

For the next half-hour Alana pushed her entire collection of fake cocks in my mouth and I correctly identified them all. She had even run in a small summer sausage, a carrot and a cucumber on me and I had nailed them all.

Then Alana said, "This next one you do not know. I just bought it a specialty shop and it was hideously expensive because of its unique features. It has the texture of real skin and it has a small sack that can be filled with warm milk that I can have the cock shoot into you by squeezing a bulb. You should know me well enough to know the name I have given it," and then it was pushed at my lips. I opened my mouth and took it in and was surprised to find that it did indeed have the texture of real skin, but what got my immediate attention was the size - it was huge! It stretched the corners of my mouth and Alana said, "My lover is now going to fuck your face until he shoots his cum into your mouth. You will swallow all of it and then if you can name him your prize will be my body."

She began to saw the dildo back and forth in my mouth, going in deeper with every stroke, and all the time crooning, "Suck it slave, suck that big, beautiful cock, suck it."

I thought that Alana was getting a little too carried away with things, but I couldn't say anything because my mouth was full. My arms and legs were tied to the chair so I couldn't push her away from me or move away from her. Suddenly Alana said, "My lover is going to cum now. Be a good slave and swallow it all." A stream of warm fluid hit the back of my throat and my first thought was that doesn't taste like any warm milk I ever had before and then I was swallowing and gagging as I tried hard to swallow all of the fluid.

"Can you name my lover slave?" and she pulled the object from my mouth.

There was a possibility, albeit a small one, that I would be wrong, but I was sure that I was right.

"Your lover's name is Tim."

"Very good slave," Alana said as she moved behind me and took off the blindfold.

I blinked my eyes a few times and then threw up all over myself. Standing in front of me, with drops of cum still hanging from his cock, was Tim. He looked down at me and sneered, "What does it feel like to have a real man's dick in your mouth." Standing ten feet behind him was Todd holding a video camera. I had just been videotaped sucking another man's cock! Alana was wiping my face and trying to clean up the mess I'd just made when I had the sudden realization that another man's cum had just gone down my throat and I threw up again.

Alana said, "You guys go on into the bedroom, I'll be there in a minute." She stuffed a clean rag in my mouth and said, "I'm sorry baby, but I've got to have that huge cock. I love you and I hope you love me enough to forgive me for what I just did to you, but I crave that monster cock between my legs. He is an arrogant, insufferable bastard, but he also has that monster cock. As long as you let him fuck me he won't show that tape to anyone. I really, really do love you baby and I'm sorry for this, but now I know how a cocaine addict feels when he can't get his fix and I've got to have Tim baby, I've just got to have him. I know you're mad now so I'm not going to untie you until they are gone, but please remember that you are the only man I love," and then she left me and walked into the bedroom.

I sat in that chair, in the stinking mess I'd made, and listened to the noises coming from the bedroom. When Tim and Todd left Tim looked at me and said, "You ain't that bad a cocksucker. The next time I come over I'll let you get me ready for your wife," and then he gave me his sneering smile as he walked out of the house.

Five minutes later Alana came out of the bedroom and began to untie me. "I love you baby, honest to God I do and I'll make it up to you, I promise," but as soon as she had me untied I shoved her away from me.

"Get out of my sight you worthless whore before I kill you" and I left the house and I haven't been back.

In the three weeks since Alana, Tim and Todd pulled their little stunt I've not spoken to her - not once - not even to take her phone calls. Other than a divorce I don't have a clue as to what I'm going to do next to get even with the three of them, but as I look out my office window I know it won't be murder. At least not yet!

***

When the idea finally came to me it had the benefit of utter simplicity. All I had to do was act normally and let the pieces fall into place.

It had been three weeks since I had walked out of the house and I had not spoken to Alana in all that time. Not because she didn't try to get in touch with me, but because I wanted nothing to do with her. I came home at three in the afternoon when I knew she would still be at work and moved myself into the spare bedroom. I was in the kitchen making myself a sandwich when Alana came home. Having seen my car in the garage she knew I was there and she came running into the house calling out my name. I ignored her as she went through the house calling out for me. She finally came into the kitchen, saw me and then she ran to me and threw her arms around me.

"Oh God baby, you're home. I've missed you terribly and I've been so worried about you."

I put my hand in the middle of her chest and gave her a hard push and she stumbled backwards into the wall.

"Just keep away from me you disgusting piece of shit."

"But you ca…"

"The only reason that I'm here is that I can't afford a divorce right now and I can't afford to make the mortgage payment on this place and keep an apartment too. Until I can find some way to financially do what needs to be done I'll be staying in the spare bedroom. I'll stay out of your way and you stay the fuck out of mine. Don't even look in my direction. The only thing I want from you is advance notice whenever you bring those two assholes over. I want to make sure that I'm not here because the temptation to do them great bodily harm would be just too great. The last thing I need is to go to jail over what I might do to them if I got my hands on them."

"Baby, I love you and you know that I do. We can wo…"

"Don't make me laugh Alana. No way anyone could do to me what you did if they loved me. If you could love me and do that I shudder to think what you might be capable of if you hated me. Just keep away from me Alana. I don't want a fucking thing from you except to be kept up to date on your schedule where those two assholes are concerned."

It wasn't that easy of course. Alana just knew that I still loved her as much as I always had and that I was just going through a period of being mad. She left little love notes lying around the place for me and she bought me presents and left them on the bed in the spare bedroom. For the first two weeks I was back Alana didn't have Todd and Tim over. I don't know if she saw them someplace else or not, but they didn't come over to our house. Alana finally accepted that I wasn't going to have anything to do with her and soon what I had been waiting for happened.

"Todd and Tim are coming over at seven-thirty tonight."

At seven I left the house, got in my car and drove off. I circled the block and parked on a side street where I could watch the front door of the house. The two of them showed up at seven-twenty and left at eleven and at one-thirty I went home. Three days later they came over and again I left and didn't go home until they were gone. I let it happen two more times to let them get over their worries that I might be waiting for them with a gun. I wanted them to feel comfortable about Alana's wimpy husband being afraid to be there when they came to visit.

Thursday night Alana let me know that they would be over at seven on Friday. I already had things arranged so at six I left the house and parked on the side street and waited. They showed up at six-fifty and I gave them twenty minutes to get to the bedroom, get naked and get into Alana and then I went back to the house and let myself in. I could hear them talking as I moved quietly up the stairs.

Tim was speaking. "And just where is the gutless wonder tonight?"

"Must you talk about him that way?"

"Hey sweets, I'm only telling it like it is. He is gutless. He let us do what we did and now he's afraid that I'll hurt him if he gives me any shit."

"He didn't let us do anything. He was already blindfolded and tied to the chair when it happened. I doubt very much you could have held him down and done it if he knew what was coming. He would have hurt you and I know it."

"All I know is that if somebody did that to me he would be buried by now."

"That's beside the point. I love him and I don't like listening to you talk that way about him."

"You love him huh? Then why do you have both hands around my cock and why are you letting Todd lick your pussy?"

Alana never got to answer that question because I stepped into the room and the three noticed me all at the same time. My sudden appearance seemed to render them speechless. Then again, maybe it was the Colt 1911-A1 that I had in my hand that grabbed their attention. I looked right at Tim and I said, "I'd have gotten to you sooner ass wipe, but it takes time to find the right gun, learn to use it and then practice enough to get good with it. But I'm here now and that's what counts, right? What were you saying about being buried by now?"

At that Tim appeared to be just a little shaken up. Alana was sitting on the bed her face pale as a sheet of paper. Todd was shaking so badly that he looked like a naked man outside in a blizzard.

Todd gulped and his voice quavered when he said, "Wha...wha... what are yo... yo... going to do?"

"You ever hear the saying that "Paybacks can be a mother fucker?" Well that is just what this is – payback! Let me explain to you how this is going to work. You are going to do what I tell you or I will use the gun on you. This is the way I see it. If I kill you no judge or jury is going to let me skate. When they find out why I killed you they might be sympathetic and let me plead down to a lesser charge, but I'd still go to jail and I don't want that. On the other hand I have every reason to believe that a jury will find me not guilty or at least let me walk with minimum penalty if all I do is fuck you up. You said it yourself Tim. If anyone had done to you what you did to me they would be buried, right? The jury will think the same way so when they see you on crutches or in a wheel chair they will just think that you got what you deserved. Paying court costs and doing 500 hours of community service in exchange for crippling you for life doesn't sound like a bad deal, now does it?"

"I don't know what you are planning, but you won't get away with it," snarled Tim.

"I just told you that I don't plan on trying to get away with it, I just plan on not paying too high a price. Here is the menu of choices. I blow away one kneecap and put you on crutches for the rest of your life. I blow away both knees and your future is a wheel chair. In addition to crutches or a wheel chair I could also blow away an elbow and make that arm useless for the rest of your life. I'll naturally pick the right one if you're right handed or the left if you are a southpaw. Are we clear on this? I don't want you dead, but I would love to have you spend the rest of your life wishing you were. So, do what you are told and survive or give me a ration of shit and don't – your choice."

Alana had tears running down her cheeks and Todd was still shaking. Tim was looking at me defiantly which is about what I had expected the arrogant asshole to do.

"Todd, go over to the closet, get the green backpack on the floor and dump the contents on the bed."

He did what I told him and three pair of handcuffs and several sections of rope cascaded down onto the bed.

"Take one set of cuffs and cuff Alana to the chair in front of her makeup table."

He did it and then I told Tim to lie down on his back on the bed.

"And if I don't?"

"I'll make you a cripple and it won't bother me a bit."

He got on his back and I told Todd to tie his wrists to the bedposts.

"That's to keep you alive Tim. I figure that you are stupid enough to try and rush me and I'd be forced to kill you. Just lie there and let Todd secure you. And Todd? I'll be checking the knots so make sure you do a good job."

When Todd was done I checked the knots and made sure that they were good and tight and then I stepped back and said, "Remember your Bible guys? Exodus 21 verses 23 to 25? "Thou shall give life for life, eye for eye, tooth for tooth" and so on? Well, what you did to me now gets done to you. You made me suck a cock so now you get to suck one too. Get on the bed Todd and put yourself in a sixty-nine position over Tim. Then the two of you suck each other off."

Todd hesitated and I said, "Okay Todd, I'll let you chose. Right knee or left" and I pulled the hammer back on the Colt and pointed it in the general direction of his knees. He scrambled to get up on the bed and into position. His cock hung down in Tim's face and Tim turned his head aside and he said, "No fucking way you cock sucker, I won't do it."

"Pity. Todd won't get much enjoyment out of sucking on a limp dick, but by the same token you may never get to use it for anything again except to pee."

I went to the closet and came back with something that looked like a policeman's nightstick. I carried it over and showed it to Tim. "This is a cattle prod. I have no idea what the lasting effects of having it touched to your cock and balls will be. Hey, you might even get a charge out of it." Then I laughed, "I think I made a funny. Get a charge out of it, get it?"

Tim just glared at me.

"No sense of humor huh?"

I looked at Todd and said, "You're not doing what I told you Todd. Get to work on Tim's cock. I'm not going to tell you again."

With a great deal of reluctance Todd bent to his task. I had to smile when I saw Tim's cock begin to grow as Todd mouthed him.

"Like those blow jobs huh? How do you know you won't enjoy giving one?"

I put the cattle prod in front of Tim's face.

"See the three little LED's? One is red, that means it has been turned on. The yellow one means that the charge is building up. When the third one turns green it means that the prod is charged up and ready to use." I flicked on the switch and the red light came on. "When that light turns green you better have Todd's cock in your mouth or I use this on you. I'll touch your balls first, then your cock and then I'll shove it up your ass. I'm told that it holds eight charges before it has to recharge and once I start on you with it I'm not stopping until it runs out of juice."

When the yellow light came on Tim gave me a look of pure hatred, but he turned his head and captured Todd's cock in his mouth. While I had been explaining the cattle prod to Tim Todd had been working on Tim's dick like his life depended on it and I'm sure that he thought that it did.

I said, "When you both have cum in the other's mouth the ordeal will be almost over" and then I walked over to stand next to Alana. She was sobbing and looking down at the floor.

"How does it feel to be tied to a chair and be helpless while somebody fucks over you?"

She kept sobbing and looked away from me. I grabbed a handful of her hair and twisted her face toward the bed, "Look at them Alana, don't they make a lovely couple?"

She sobbed out, "What are you going to do to me?"

"In time Alana, in time. I won't neglect you, I promise."

On the bed Tim and Todd were working on each other's joints. Todd was getting into it. I don't know that sucking Tim's cock was doing much for him, but he sure like his cock being in Tim's mouth. Todd's hips were moving up and down as he fucked Tim's face and I wondered if their friendship would survive the night. Who knows, they just might have found something that might keep them home and off the streets? Suddenly Todd groaned and he came in Tim's mouth. Tim gagged and choked, but he was tied down and couldn't move so he had to swallow. Tim was mouthing Todd's limp cock, but I don't think that he knew he was doing it as all his feelings seem to be in his cock. He was humping his hips up off the bed and driving his cock into Todd's mouth and I unlocked Alana's handcuffs and told her to go over and untie Tim. As soon as his hands were free he sat up and grabbed the back of Todd's head with both hands and held on tight while he shot into Todd's mouth. I saw cum drip from Todd's lips as Tim emptied his balls.

I gave them a minute to catch their breath and then I told Todd to take the two pair of handcuffs and cuff himself to Tim. "Your right wrist to his left and then take the other cuff and put it on your left wrist."

"Why? We did what you told us."

"All that did was make us even. Now we get to the revenge part. Don't worry, it won't be painful; humiliating maybe, but not painful."

Todd did what I told him to do and then I had the two men walk into the bathroom and get in the bathtub. I told Todd to take the free end of the handcuff on his left wrist and lock it tight around the faucet handle. When he had done that I tucked the Colt behind my belt, unzipped myself and took out my cock.

"I've been saving this for hours," I said, and then I pissed all over the both of them. When I was done I turned to Alana, "Your turn now Alana. Dry them off."

She reached for a towel, but I took it out of her hands. "No towel Alana, use your tongue."

She recoiled at that, "Oh no, I won't do that."

"Your choice Alana, but I can tell you this much. You won't have much of a sex life if you are confined to a wheel chair."

I pulled the Colt from where I had tucked it in and I had just pulled back the hammer when she said, "All right, okay, I'll do it."

"Get to it then."

"Do you really hate me that much?"

"I hate what you did to me and that's enough."

The tears started falling again, but she got in the tub and went to work. She stopped twice to toss her cookies, but I waved the gun at her and she went back to work. When she was done I had her use the cuffs that Todd had cuffed her to the chair with to cuff herself to Tim.

"Okay children, I have one last thing to take care of. Don't go away."

I left the bathroom and came back a few minutes later with a video camera. "I had this hidden so that it would catch all the action. I can edit out the ropes. So, now we each have a tape. If the one you have never sees the light of day neither will this one, but if I even hear a rumor that there is a tape of me out there I will put this on the Internet so fast it will make your head swim and I'll make damned sure that everyone that I know who knows the both of you will also get a copy."

"We can trade," Todd said, "The tape we have for that one."

"No we can't. I would never trust that you didn't make copies. I'll just hang on to this one. If you are smart you will destroy the one you have to make damned sure it doesn't get found inadvertently and get out."

"But you'll still have yours. How do we know we can trust you?"

"You don't. You just have to hope, but think of this; I could have hurt you both bad tonight, but I didn't. The other thing to remember is that you guys started this, not me."

I turned to leave and Alana said, "Where are you going?"

"Away from this place."

"But you can't just go and leave us here."

"You're right, I can't. It could be days before anyone finds you."

I took out my cell phone and when the police dispatcher answered I gave the address and reported seeing two men trying to break in.

"There! Help is on the way. You all take care now" and I left the house.

That was a week ago and Alana has called my office and cell phone a dozen times a day since. So far I haven't taken the calls, but I do have to admit to a touch of curiosity. What could she possibly have to say to me now?

~The End~

Watch out for the next volume in Just Plain Bob's
Erotica Short Stories Series

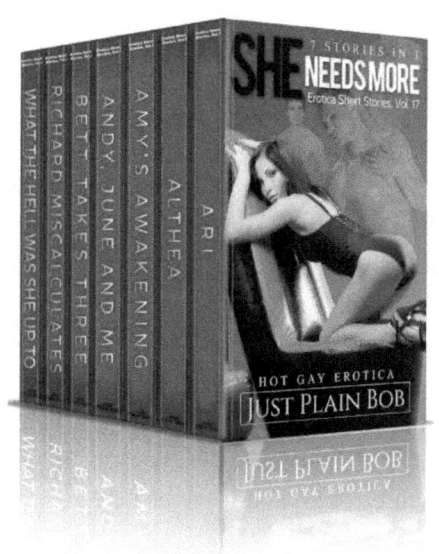

Also by this Author:

The Prodigal Family: The Abbotts

Watching My Shared Wife

The Waitress and the Runaway Husband

Baiting Mr. Little

Too Hot for Henry

Chuck's Fantasy

The Redhead's Desires

Rescued at Riley's

His Every Fantasy

Open Mike Night

Pursuit for Revenge

Why Does He Do That?

Halloween & Drugs

Tracey

When Rob Met Kari

Becoming a Shared Wife, Vol. 1 –
(Wife Sharing and Other Adventures)

Becoming a Shared Wife, Vol. 2 –
(Hazardous Wives)

Becoming a Shared Wife, Vol. 3 –
(Wives Who Stray)

Becoming a Shared Husband, Vol. 1 –

(Suck Me)

Becoming a Shared Husband, Vol. 2 –

(Husbands Who Stray)

Becoming a Shared Husband, Vol. 3 –

(Get even!)

Becoming a Shared Couple, Vol. 1 –

(Steamy Swingers)

Becoming a Shared Couple, Vol. 2 –

(The Share Thing)

Becoming a Shared Couple, Vol. 3 –

(Kathy is Wild)

Erotica Short Stories, Vol. 1 –

(Taboo Desires)

Erotica Short Stories, Vol. 2 –

(Nasty Steps)

Erotica Short Stories, Vol. 3 –

(Married But…)

Erotica Short Stories, Vol. 4 –

(Sizzling 10)

Erotica Short Stories, Vol. 5 –

(In My Wife's Panties)

Erotica Short Stories, Vol. 6 –

(Taboo Unlimited Desires)

Erotica Short Stories, Vol. 7 –

(XXX Stories)

From the Author

WANT FREE COPIES OF MY BOOKS?

Just visit my blog and download free copies of my books:

awesomeauthors.org/justplainbob

If you enjoyed any of my books then please share the love and promote my books in Amazon.

If you write me a review and send me an email I will send you a free book, or many.

(Just know that these emails are filtered by my publisher.)

Good news is always welcome.

One Last Thing, For Kindle Readers...

When you turn the page, Kindle will give you the opportunity to rate this book and share your thoughts on Facebook and Twitter. If you enjoyed my writings, would you please take a few seconds to let your friends know about it? Because... when they enjoy they will be grateful to you and so will I.

Thank You!

An Open Letter from Just Plain Bob

A message for those who like my stories, those who hate my stories, those who are indifferent and those who have yet to make up their minds.

I have often stated that I really don't care what others think about my stories, that I write for my own enjoyment and then I offer to share. If you like my stories fine and if you don't, also fine since I have already satisfied my target audience - me!

It is human nature to strive to get better. If you take up bowling your first games are going low scoring, but you will work and practice to get better and as your average climbs you may forget the game where you had three gutter balls and shot an eighty-six, but that game is still there in your past.

Your first time on the golf course you shot an eighty on the front nine, but did you settle for that being your game or did you work to improve? You may eventually get a three handicap, but that nine hole eighty is still there as part of your past.

When you hired in at your job did you say, "Cool, I got it made" and do nothing more than what you barely had to do or did you go to work thinking that, "Someday I'm going to be running this place." You might never climb that high, but human nature says that you are going to at least try.

It is the same with authors who write stories and post them on sites like Literotica. Their first stories might not be all that good, but comments and feedback along with a desire to get better drive them toward putting out a better product or to at least try.

I'm no different. My first stories might not have been all that great, but they are still there on the hard drive. I like cheating wife stories and five years ago I found my first adult site that catered to cheating wife stories. It was a pay site, but it had a policy of giving a free lifetime membership to anyone who submitted five stories to the site. How hard can that be I said to myself as I sat down and fired up the word processor and went to work.

I sent my five stories in and sat back to enjoy my free membership and a funny thing happened. I started getting feedback, most of it positive, and I became hooked. I started cranking out more stories. The site I was sending my stories to had seven categories:

Bisexual
Cream Pie

Groups
I Watch
Gang Bang
Racial
SM/BD

I know nothing about bisexual or SM/BD and I had no interest in Groups so all the stories I wrote I tailored for the four remaining categories:

Cream Pie
I Watch
Gang Bang
Racial.

I turned out eight stories a month, two for each category, which means that after five years I have over 120 stories in each of those categories and they are all still on the hard drive.

A year ago I received an email asking me why I never posted stories on Literotica. The answer? I didn't know about Lit. I pulled it up, liked what I saw, and started sending in stories to it. All new stories? No, not hardly, not with over 400 stories sitting on the hard drive. Maybe one new story for each fifteen or so old ones. The newer ones are better, at least I think they are and I have received some feedback that leads me to believe that others think so too, and I will continue to write new ones.

But I am still going to recycle what is on the hard drive, stories that were written specifically to fit the four categories. That means that those of you who hate cream pie stories still have eighty or so to look forward to. Ditto for those who call me a racist; you will get another seventy or so interracial stories.

Those who hate wimps will only see about fifty more of those because the stories I sent to the I Watch category were split 50/50 between what some call wimps and some call "real men." Why the 50/50 split? It came from listening to the readers. I would get feedback asking me why all the men in my stories were hard asses. "In real life men are more forgiving, especially if it is the first indiscretion." So I would write stories with forgiving husbands and boyfriends and then the next batch of feedback would say, "Why are all your husbands spineless wimps" and I'd write stories that went back the other way.

Eventually I came to realize that I was wasting my time - there was no way I could write a story that would satisfy everybody and that is when I adopted my philosophy of writing for my own enjoyment and then offering to share.

As far as the gangbang stories? Well, what can I say? Gangbangs are gangbangs and there are still eighty or so of them to go.

The bottom line is that Literotica readers are going to see more of my old stories than my new ones. If I'm still around three or four years from now it will probably go the other way, more new than old.

I feel the need to respond to some of the comments and emails I have received. By far the largest percentage comes from people who say, "You are an asshole because all women are not whores and sluts and that's all you make them out to be."

Next most common is, "You must really hate women you sick fuck."

"You must be a wimp because all the men in your stories are wimps" is up there in the top ten along with, "Why don't you give it a rest and go crawl off in a hole somewhere."

There is a lot more, but I'm only going to address those four and in reverse order.

I won't stop and go crawl in a hole because I am enjoying the hell out of what I am doing and remember what I said, I am doing this for MY OWN ENJOYMENT and then I offer to share. Some obviously like my sharing with them and so I will continue to do so. No one is holding a gun to a reader's head and telling them they must click on a Just Plain Bob story or die. It is a conscious choice on the reader's part to move that mouse and click on that story.

When a man finds out he has a cheating wife or girlfriend there are only a limited number of ways he can handle it. If he loves her he can forgive, try to forget and try to hold on and somehow make things work. He can turn his back on her, walk away and get on with his life. The third option is to take revenge.

According to a good portion of those who send me feedback the first and second options are proof that the men are wimps. If the man takes the third option he is still considered a wimp if he doesn't do some sort of physical damage to the woman and her lover. These readers believe that the only way not to be a wimp is to kill, maim and destroy everything in sight. Doing that however, will invariably get the man throw in jail and that is why it so rarely happens in real life.

In real life most revenge takes place in the man's head when he says to himself, "I should have _____ (fill in the blank) the fucking cunt!" I know this because I have been there and done that (see The Dark Trilogy). In my stories I try to mirror real life so kill, maim and destroy are going to be for the most part absent. Outside of some fisticuffs there will be very little physical violence in my stories. Most of my husbands are going to do what I did, what several of my friends and others that I know have done, forgive, or walk away. If this makes them wimps and me a wimp for writing the story that way, so be it.

Next is the "I must hate all women." Nothing could be farther from the truth. I love women. I lust after women. I even like whores and sluts. I have been married four times, engaged two other times (that did not end in marriage) and I have always had girlfriends between marriages. My philosophy is that women were put on this earth for me to enjoy and I'm not talking just sexually. I could sit at the mall (and have) for hours and just girl watch.

The engagements, girlfriends and three of the four marriages bring me to the #1 anti JPB comment on the list.

"You are an asshole because all women aren't whores and sluts."

Well dear reader, you can not prove that by me! I will say up front that I KNOW all women aren't whores and sluts, BUT the majority of the women in my life were. My mother ran around on my father for years while he was driving a truck for a living. My Aunt Margaret cheated regularly on my Uncle Bill, as did my Aunt Mildred on my Uncle Paul. My Aunt Betty fucked around on my Uncle Bob for years and finally left him for his brother, my Uncle Wendell. Uncle Wendell in turn caught her on her knees at his company Christmas party giving Season's Greetings to his boss.

My sister is three times divorced and each divorce came about when the then current husband caught her out spreading pollen. Both of the engagements I mentioned ended when I found out that I was not the one and only and a lot of the girls I dated between marriages never made it to engagement status for the same reason.

And that brings me to my three ex-wives. The first one, Helen (I believe I commented on her in the intro to The Dark Trilogy) had seven different lovers before I found out what was going on. I was living proof that love is blind. Ditto with my second wife. She had a secret life that she hid from me and when I found out about her brother, his friends and the gangbangs she was history.

My third marriage ended in divorce because of a different kind of cheating (and I can just imagine the outrage I am going to get over this) - she cheated on me with an idea. I was away from home on business, she was lonely, a couple of Jehovah's Witnesses knocked on the door and my wife, with nothing better to do invited them in. When I came home from my trip I found out that she had found God. On a scale that runs from TRUE BELIEVER on one end to ATHEIST on the other you will find me just to the right of AGNOSTIC and since I would not allow myself to be SAVED the marriage eventually died.

So yes, I write about sluts and whores because as everyone knows, you tend to write about the things you know. And I do like sluts and whores, just not the ones that lie to me and cheat on me.

So be forewarned - if you click on a Just Plain Bob story you will be getting sluts, whores and husbands who do not kill, maim and destroy. There are other things you will rarely find in a Just Plain Bob story. Even though I try to mirror real life my stories all take place in StoryLand. In StoryLand STDs and unwanted pregnancies do not exist unless the author feels like they may add something to the story. Bad things do not happen in StoryLand unless the author so wills it and no amount of "You should have..." in comments and feedback will change a story already posted.

Lastly, I will touch on a truth. None of what I have written here means shit because the same readers will still read the same stories that they profess to hate and make the same comments they have always made. Knowing this, I will deliberately post stories that will have them frothing at the mouth.

It is the least I can do for an adoring public.

Thank you!

Just Plain Bob
justplainbob@awesomeauthors.org

You may also like the books by these authors:

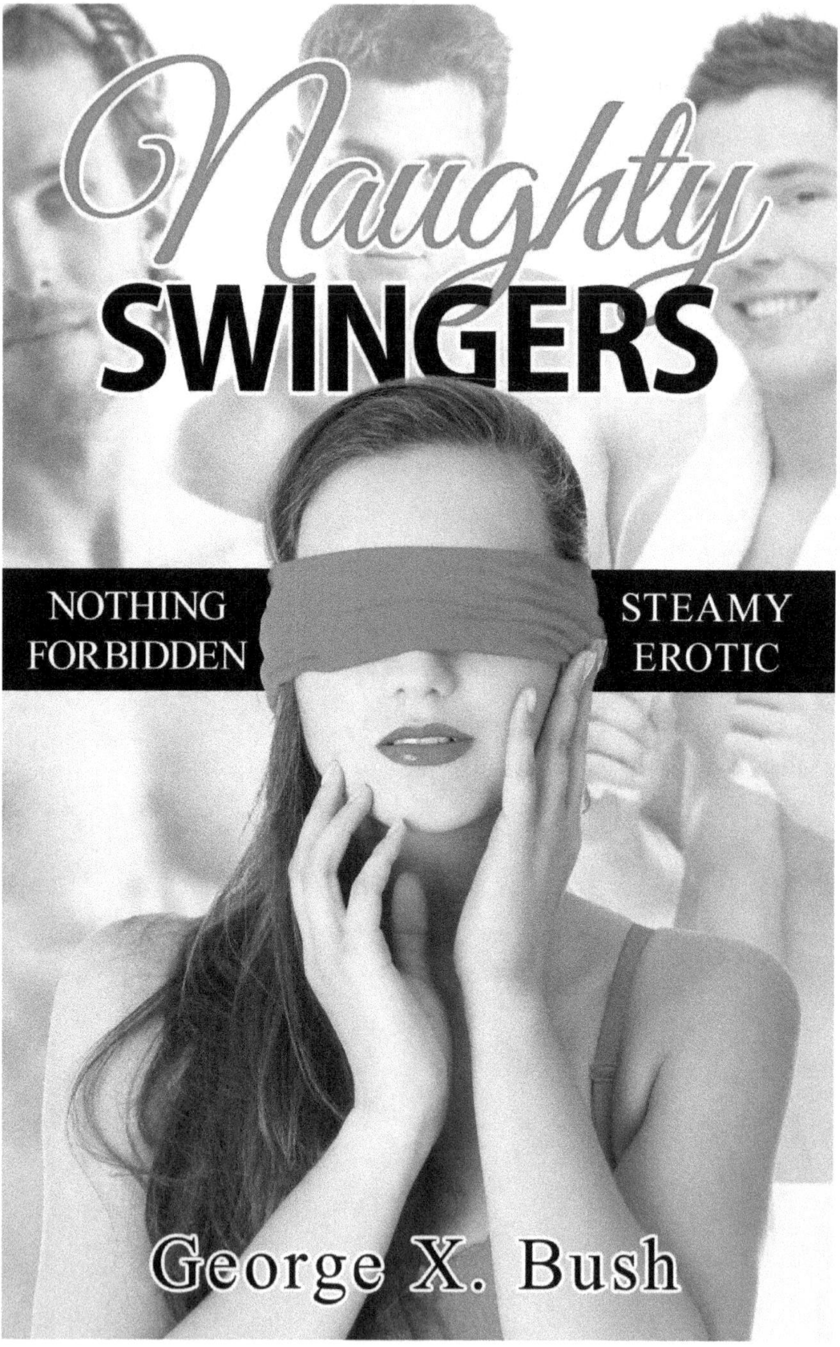
Naughty
SWINGERS
NOTHING
FORBIDDEN
STEAMY
EROTIC
George X. Bush

"Why don't we go out tonight?" Adam suggested to his wife, Keri.

"If you want to," Keri agreed. "Any special reason or place in mind?"

"Actually, yes," Adam replied. "It's a special sort of place, private."

"What's it like?" Keri asked, intrigued.

"I don't really know, except that there are special costume requirements for women," Adam told her. "I heard about it at work from some of the guys."

"What kind of special requirements?" Keri asked.

"A special mask," Adam explained.

"Where do we get it?" Keri inquired.

"Well, actually one of the guys gave me one, just in case, you know," he replied lamely.

"So, let's see it," Keri said, crooking her head sideways as she looked at her husband.

Slowly Adam reached into his briefcase and withdrew the mask.

"Oh, my," Keri said, her eyes widening in surprise as she reached for it. "This is different," she commented as she held it up and looked at it. "What is this supposed to be?" she asked, indicating a mouthpiece-like part with a ball on the other end.

"You put that part in your mouth," Adam explained.

"How do you know this?" Keri asked, a twinkle in her eye.

"They showed me how it works," Adam told her. "I didn't know either."

"So show me," Keri told him, holding it out.

"Well, it's like this," Adam said, reaching up and pulling the mask over her head. It covered her eyes and nose with the mouthpiece filling her mouth. There was a good-sized hole through the mouthpiece making it possible to breath. Adam fastened the laces in the back and tightened the mask. Now Keri couldn't see or talk and Adam noticed that her breathing rate was increasing. Keri reached up with her hands and felt around the mask, feeling the soft leather and trying to control her panic at having been stricken blind and dumb in one fell swoop. When she reached behind her head for the laces, Adam quickly untied them and helped her out of the mask.

"Wow, that's some sensation," Keri said when Adam had removed the mask. "And I'd have to wear that?"

"That's the rules," Adam told her. "If you take it off you have to leave."

"Wow! It sounds really strange," she said. "Is this something that you want to do?" Keri asked him.

"Only if you want to," Adam told her. "It sounded pretty kinky to me when they told me about it."

"They've been, obviously," Keri commented. "How did their wives like it?"

"Well, he said they'd been back since, so I guess she did," Adam replied.

"Well, if you'll take good care of me I'll go and see what it's like," Keri said, smiling at him. "What else should I wear?"

"Well, I heard there's dancing, so something comfortable for that."

"It'll be strange dancing blind," Keri commented. "But it could also be sort of neat too, I guess. Let's go change," she said, turning towards their bedroom.

It only took them about ten minutes to dress. Keri wore what she usually wore to go out dancing, a short skirt and a halter top. Her full breasts filled the halter top and her skirt came only one third of the way down her thighs. She had nice long legs and she knew she looked good. Instead of her usual high heels, though, she was wearing a pair of sensible flat shoes.

"Dancing blind, you know," she said in way of explanation.

"You look great," Adam told her, meaning it.

He thought she was the hottest looking woman on the planet and he loved it when she dressed hot to go out. As they went to the car and began driving to the party, Adam was filled with trepidation. There was more about the party that he knew that he hadn't told Keri about. He'd had this secret desire for a long time and hadn't known how to act on it until now. He just hoped that Keri would go along and not freak out.

It only took them about 20 minutes to get to where they were going, a big beautiful house in the section of the city reserved for very rich people. Keri was suitably impressed as they turned into the drive and saw about a dozen other cars already parked there. When they parked, Adam pulled out the mask and held it out to her.

"Are you sure you want to do this?" he asked once more.

"Why not?" Keri asked, taking it from him. "What's the worst that can happen?"

If you enjoyed this sample then look for **Naughty Swingers**.

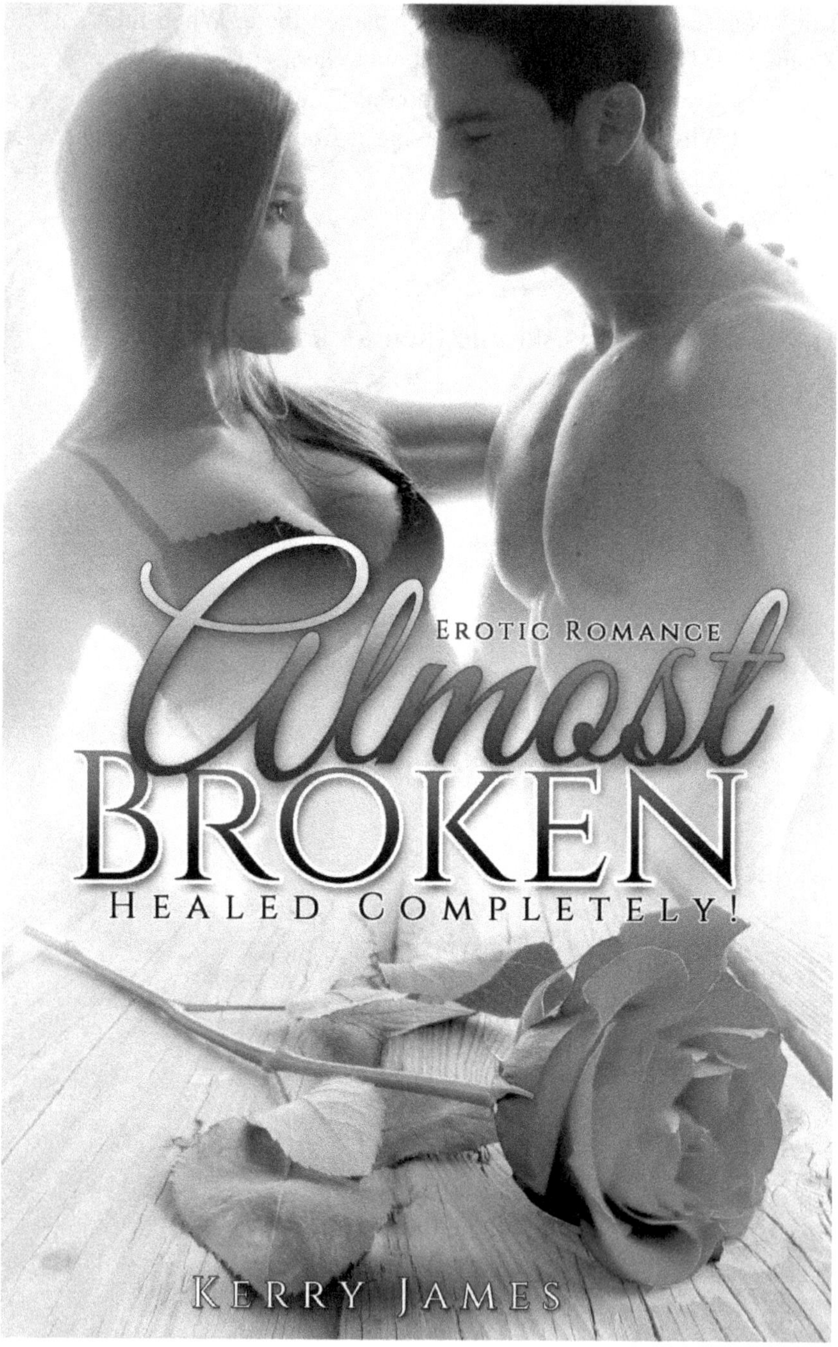
EROTIC ROMANCE
Almost
BROKEN
HEALED COMPLETELY!
KERRY JAMES

Where does life take us? Why is it that when you have settled on one course, fate comes knocking at your door and takes you off on a tangent? That's what happened to me, it seems to keep happening to me. I get used to my life, and then fate throws a surprise my way. Sometimes it is a little tap-tap on the door, at others it's a loud knock. Sometimes it blows the door open, and when it is really serious fate just takes the thing off with its hinges.

I am Jack Hunter. My life to date had been particularly uneventful, although that would depend on your point of view. I had a wife, and a daughter. I also had an affair which while it didn't become the reason for my divorce, soured me sufficiently to seek to split with my wife. I will hold my hand up and acknowledge that I cheated on my wife. Not a good thing to do, but I will say in my defence that because my wife was in love with the bottle; Vodka and Tonic was her favourite so no one could be actually sure whether she was tippling or not; our love life was virtually zero. It's no easy task to make love to someone who reeks of alcohol. Brenda, my wife didn't appear to be bothered by our lack of intimacy, her next drink was far more important. I tried to get her to admit the problem, her Doctor tried, her mother tried, even our daughter, Libby, only three years old but she understood that something was wrong with mummy. Nothing worked. Despair and frustration were taking my self-esteem to new depths so when I had met a rather lovely lady called Deborah it quickly went from acquaintance to friendship to lovers. Our affair went on for three years. But when I called quits on my marriage, and as you would expect got taken to the cleaners in the resulting divorce, Deborah made it plain that we were not going to be an item. She came round for the sex but nothing else. Sounds like any man's dream, doesn't it? I had sex on tap and no emotional baggage to go with it. But I was one of those men who wanted emotion in a relationship, so eventually I told her it was over.

The legal process in the UK was slow but exacting. It had however problems in making its judgments effective. I had visiting rights with my daughter, which were denied or delayed for spurious reasons. My solicitor would petition the court again and again to enforce the judgment. The court would confirm the judgment but never took action to ensure it was complied with. So slowly I lost touch with my daughter.

I met Jasmine in a supermarket; I actually helped her with the heavy bags. We had coffee, then dinner and eventually we started sleeping together on occasional nights. We went on like this for five years, until one day I got a fixed penalty speeding fine in the post. The location was not one I had driven through for months, so I queried the penalty. The bloody camera was right, it was my car, but at the time I had been away at a trade show, and I had travelled to the show by train. There was only one person who had access to my house, and the keys to the company car. Jasmine! After a lot of heated arguments she admitted she had 'borrowed' the car. Problem was that she was not insured to drive it, a criminal offence in the UK. If she admitted the offence to the police, chances were that she would certainly be banned from driving, and get a hefty fine. There was also an outside chance of a prison sentence. I paid the fine, took the points on my licence, and Jasmine became history.

A few months after that lesson, I was invited to a party at a friend's house, which was where I met Bridget. We were under no illusions that we had been invited by well-meaning friends who thought that being single was an offence against nature. Well we did hit it off. Remaining friends for nearly ten years, but the tingle was just not there.

If you enjoyed this sample then look for **Almost Broken**.

Dear Ms. Joan:

This is the report you asked me to write up about me, my husband and our very dear friend (and special family member), Maria.

Let me begin by telling you about each of us.

About me (Annette)... Since the first time I had intercourse in the backseat of a boyfriend's car, I have always enjoyed the feelings of pleasure that sex has given me. While I had feelings of conflict over the non-marital sex those first few times, I still enjoyed the feel of a man's organ probing around inside me. Then I learned to give my dates manual and oral pleasure. I found that I liked that too.

A few years later one of the guys I dated treated me to "head." I was hesitant at first to let him do that, but he insisted. The intense pleasure of that experience left me wanting "head" as often as a date would give it to me.

That was my sexual background prior to meeting Jordan (or Jordy, as I call him). From our earliest dates, we made sex a regular part of our dates. Six months after we met, we married. At the time, Jordy was 24 and I was 23.

Oh yes, the obligatory physical description. I stand 5' 6" tall, generally weigh about 130 lbs., and have rather full C-cup boobs. My eyes are blue, and my hair is a sort of dishwater blond. I generally keep my hair curled and styled. While I have always thought of myself as sort of average, Jordy is constantly telling me that I am "really good lookin' with beautiful legs and tits." Who am I to disagree with him?

Both Jordy and I are college grads with post-grad degrees. For the past several years I have been doing contract engineering work out of our home. My field of engineering allows me to get work rather easily, and choose between part time or full time work.

About Jordy... Jordy is very handsome (in my subjective opinion, but Maria says so too). He stands 5' 9" tall, typically weighs about 170 lbs., and has brown hair and brown eyes. He has a ruddy complexion, a mustache and a full beard. Jordy sports a cock that when stimulated measures 8" long and 5" around. Unlike most other men I have seen, his dick tapers from a relatively small head to its thick girth (gives wonderful sensations as it enters and slides within my pussy!).

Both Jordy and I generally work full time. He works for a computer firm that sells and services software for specialty retailing businesses. His work often takes him out on the road (up to 1,000 miles away). We are both typical Anglo-Saxon Caucasians.

About Maria... Maria is a beautiful young woman (four years younger than me). Her father was half black and half American Indian. Her mother was mostly Spanish (her mother from Mexico and father from Brazil).

The result of their union was a sexy gal who has soft skin that boasts the appearance of a year-round deep Coppertone tan. Jordy says her skin looks (and tastes like) golden honey.

She has small cone-shaped breasts with large (very sensitive) nipples. Her legs are at least as long as mine, yet she just stands just 5'3" tall. Jordy describes her as "a compact gal whose legs go all the way to 'heaven'". The little nymph typically weighs in at a scant 105 lbs.

Maria was born in Porto Rico, and grew up in New Jersey. Her father died when she was very young. Her mother struggled to raise her and her two older sisters. When they grew up, the sisters left home, and really have not made much of themselves. Maria saw that, and determined that she was going to get some higher education and make something of herself.

They both also had very unsatisfying marriages to husbands who were abusive. Maria's mother got sick when Maria was just 17, and Maria decided to stay living at home and help her mother.

Meanwhile, Maria enrolled at a local community college while staying at home to care for her mother.

Her mother died just after Maria turned 20. With nothing holding her back any more, and no desire to hook up with some guy just to get married, Maria decided to travel west to begin a new life. Her savings took her only to Oklahoma City where she got work in a restaurant. After several months, she decided she didn't like Oklahoma City. She had accumulated enough money for a bus ticket to Santa Fe, New Mexico, where we happened to be living at the time.

Again, Maria took work waiting tables in a restaurant. That's where we met her, three weeks after her arrival. While dining at the restaurant where she was working, we got to talking with her. We found her to be quite attractive, pleasantly personable, and quite intelligent. She agreed to meet us for a drink after her shift ended.

We walked down the street to a nearby lounge where we each had a few drinks and got to know each other. We learned that Maria had her 21st birthday the week before, so we asked her if she would like to celebrate by joining us for a late night dip at a nearby hot springs. She said she did not have her swimsuit with her. I let her know that the place has several pools, some of which were "clothing optional," and that we seldom wore swim suits there. After giggling a bit about that prospect, she agreed, and we all piled into our car for the short trip.

I should tell you that Maria has long, straight, shiny black hair that hangs about 5" below her shoulders. Her eyes are also pools of deep black. In spite of her father's racial background, Maria's face and hair give no indication of her Black heritage. Only her skin evidences her mixed heritage... and does so in a highly attractive way.

As she and I stripped in the dressing room, I noticed she had a full, untrimmed bush covering her crotch. We both used our towels to cover ourselves on the short walk to the pool that Jordy had picked out. We slipped in on either side of him, and began to chat like we had been long-time friends. During our time in the pool, a few others joined us for a while. When I sat on the edge of the pool to cool off, Maria joined me with no evidence of concern about her nudity in the dim light.

During our conversations we let Maria know that we had a sort of open marriage, and had each occasionally enjoyed having others as sex partners. She just took it all in without any particular reaction.

Getting to Know Maria... At the end of the evening we took Maria to her apartment and made arrangements for the three of us to go out together again the following Saturday night. That night Jordy and I made passionate love as I told him that no other woman had ever turned me on before... but that Maria had. He suggested that just maybe, Maria might be a woman we could both enjoy... while giving her pleasure.

If you enjoyed this sample then look for <u>And Maria Makes Three</u>.

The Daring Doppelgangers

Hot Taboo Erotica

Jack Ryder

I saw her as I was pulling into the Pendleton truck stop. Even though it was unseasonably warm, it was still out of the ordinary for anyone to be wearing such short cutoff jeans. As my eyes travelled up the rest of her body, it was easy to see that she was a knock out. My jaw dropped when I finally studied her face. This girl could be an identical clone of that Claudia Black who was on that hit TV show Farscape.

Even with the dark aviator sun glasses she was wearing, I could swear they looked identical.

I tried not to stare at her when I passed her going in the door to buy some coffee and use the restroom.

I could not see her eyes through the dark sunglasses, but she seemed to have a whimsical smirk on her face as I went past her. I made it a point to keep my eyes on her face but I could still feel a wiggle down between my legs as I caught a whiff of her honeysuckle scented perfume. I was disappointed to find that she had left the sales area when I came back out to get my coffee and a snack cake.

She was standing by the curb as I was pulling out of the parking area. I saw two cars stop almost instantly but she waved them away just before I reached the exit driveway. I almost bit my tongue when I pulled up in front of her to see if she would accept a ride. I figured that was why she had her thumb out. Her black leather biker style jacket was completely unzipped in front and I could see most of both her big firm breasts.

When I pressed the button to lower the passenger window, she bent forward to peer in at me.

"Where do you need to go?" I asked her. I could not keep myself from glancing at her bare chest. "My breasts need to get as far away from here as possible," she taunted me when I glanced up into her eyes. "The rest of me would like to go along as well."

If you enjoyed this sample then look for **The Daring Doppelgangers**.

I could remember exactly when I knew my marriage to Jocelyn was over. It was the night of our tenth wedding anniversary. I came home early, brought flowers, and a nice silver pendant, that I knew she would wear. We kissed perfunctorily at the kitchen door, before I went upstairs to shower and change, prior to taking her out to her favorite restaurant for dinner.

What made it memorable is that we spoke hardly a word to each other, despite the fact that we had not seen or talked to each other since the previous evening. I typically left for work an hour before Jocelyn, and she was in the shower when I pulled out of the driveway that morning. At the restaurant, there were no reminiscences of past times together, no fond remembrances...nothing. We made the odd comment about the weather or our work, but nothing intimate. When we went to bed, I reached for her, hoping for at least some anniversary lovemaking, but she said she was too tired and that was that.

I lay on my back and knew then that it was over. We had each been pretending that our marriage was still alive. I thought back and realized, I wasn't even sure if we were ever in love with each other. We went through the motions, but I couldn't remember a moment when I knew for sure that I would do anything for her: walk through fire, slay dragons, or take on a gang of villains. It was a dispiriting thought, and with our life having sunk into ennui over the past two or three years, I knew a decision was at hand.

I delayed leaving for work the next morning. I might as well face it when I knew what I wanted to say. Jocelyn came down and was obviously surprised to see me sitting at the kitchen table with a coffee and the morning paper.

"What are you still doing here?" she asked, curious, as she poured her first coffee.

"I wanted to talk to you. It seemed like the best opportunity," I said quietly.

I suppose it was my tone of voice that alerted her. She looked at me, and then picked up her coffee, and sat in her usual chair.

"What did you want to talk about?" She was clearly uncomfortable with the uncertainty.

"Jocelyn, there's no easy way to say this. I will file for divorce early next week."

I watched her eyes grow large and heard the sharp intake of breath.

"Why?" she struggled to ask.

"I think you know the answer to that, as well as I do. Our marriage is dead. It died a long slow death, but it is dead," I said solemnly.

She sat silently, looking at me, thinking about what she had just heard. Slowly, she lowered her gaze to her untouched coffee, and stared at it for a few moments.

"I'm sorry, Lee. I wish it had worked. I'm sorry," she finally whispered.

"I know. Don't blame yourself. Sometimes … sometimes it just doesn't …." I couldn't finish the thought. I saw a tear, and then another trickle down her cheek.

"I'll look after the paperwork. If we use the do-it-yourself forms, we can cut the legal costs … unless you want to contest it," I said, almost as an afterthought.

"No … I won't fight it. You're right … it just didn't come out the way we wanted it to."

I stood up, kissed her cheek, and left quietly for the garage and off to work.

If there is such a thing as an amicable divorce, we were the model. It was civil and civilized. We split everything almost 50-50. Jocelyn's income was very healthy as an assistant director in the provincial government Ministry of Environment. Thus, there would be no alimony. We agreed to sell the house and close the mortgage. Our home in Burnaby was valued at an almost ridiculous amount, after the eight plus years that we had owned it. After we retired the mortgage, we split nearly three hundred thousand dollars. We both had our own retirement savings plans, and maintained them in our own names.

Jocelyn kept her car, but I drove a company lease car with no asset value to me. I let Jocelyn keep most of the furniture, except for a couple of pieces that had come from my parents and grandparents. I guess, all told, she would have taken away thirty-thousand or so in value more than me, but in truth, I really didn't care. I just wanted the whole unhappy episode to be over.

We met once more, just before the divorce was final, to make sure that there were no outstanding issues to be resolved. We chose a pub not far from our former residence, and found a semi-secluded place to talk. It didn't take us long to determine that there was nothing left to discuss, except our feelings and our future.

"So, where are you going to live?" she finally asked.

"I don't know. I quit my job last week. I'll be finished at the end of the month, and then I'm going to do what the Aussies do; 'go walkabout.'"

"I almost envy you. I wouldn't mind a sabbatical myself. I hope you find what you're looking for," she said sincerely.

"Me too. I just hope I'll know it when I find it. What about you … where are you going to live?"

"I've taken a job in the Ministry of Industry and I'm moving to Victoria. I found an apartment there. I'll enjoy that, I think. Less pressure than Environment."

"Good … I'm glad," I said honestly.

"Regrets?" she asked.

"Sure. Plenty. I wonder if it would have turned out differently if I hadn't been sterile. I'm sure that must have hurt you more than you let on, finding out after we were married. I know it hurt me. Not good for the male ego."

"Yes … it hurt. But then, we talked about adoption and IVF. We had choices. I'm not sure that would have made a big difference except that maybe we might have hung on a lot longer because of the kids, and then become much more unhappy. Not much of a choice in my opinion."

"I suppose you're right. Well," I said, raising my mug, "here's to a better future for us. I wish you all the best, Jocelyn."

She touched her wine glass to my mug and offered a faint smile. A few minutes later, we hugged and kissed each other for the last time. I stood and watched, as she slowly worked her way out of the pub, and into the parking lot. I slumped back in my seat, waiting for the waitress to come around so that I could order another beer. I didn't have any place special to go, and I was in no hurry to get there.

I moved in with my folks for a couple of weeks after the sale of the house. They were very generous and sympathetic. Mom and Dad were married over forty years, and I think they were deeply disappointed at my divorce. I had failed at something important, and I think they knew that I was ashamed to admit it. They said nothing directly to me, but I could tell by some of their inferences what they were thinking. The sooner I hit the road, the better off they would be.

There was only another week until the end of the month and my employment. I think they were surprised and dubious about my unplanned future, but they said nothing to discourage me. On a bright and sunny Saturday morning of March, I loaded the last of my bags into my car, kissed and hugged my folks, and drove off into the sunrise. I had absolutely no idea where I was going, but I really wasn't worried about it.

If you enjoyed this sample then look for **Casual Encounters**.

WANT FREE COPIES OF MY BOOKS?
Just visit my blog and download free copies of my books:
awesomeauthors.org/justplainbob